Blood
Ice

J. Mykle Levitt

iUniverse, Inc.
Bloomington

Blood Ice

iUniverse books may be ordered through booksellers or by contacting:

*iUniverse
1663 Liberty Drive
Bloomington, IN 47403
www.iuniverse.com
1-800-Authors (1-800-288-4677)*

*ISBN: 978-1-4697-8720-6 (sc)
ISBN: 978-1-4697-8721-3 (hc)
ISBN: 978-1-4697-8722-0 (e)*

Library of Congress Control Number: 2012903391

Printed in the United States of America

iUniverse rev. date: 3/27/2012

Special Thanks to Ron Daniels

To: Zoe and Alfi

Chapter One

On the third floor of the abandoned warehouse festooned with peeling paint and dust-ridden floors, the old man stood in front of the broken panes, waiting. His Fedora covered his head. His wool coat covered his body.. His glove-covered hands lay to his sides, showing his diamond cufflinks, which enhanced his shirt. His shoes shone glossy; his face worn. He was watching, waiting, for soon it would be done and he could concentrate on his true mission—a mission that began years before.

Then a young, muscular man with a large, oblong bag slung over his shoulder came into the old man's focus from across the street. The bag bobbed with each jogging step he took in the late-October rain. He headed for the alley that housed the entrance to the warehouse and then came into the warehouse from its side.

The elevator's hum came to the third floor, then stopped. with a clatter. The old man heard footsteps coming up behind him across the floor. The old man didn't turn. He didn't look. He didn't need to. He knew what was in the bag, and he felt a smirk growing on his face. The young man walked across the creaking floor and dropped the bag with a thud next to the old man. Then he stood, awaiting his next orders.

"Goot," the old man said as he turned to look at his prize. "Open de bag."

The young man unzipped the bag, and a smile from the old man took the place of his smirk; either way, his features looked treacherous at best. The old man's eyes twinkled. The first leg of his plans was almost finished. From his pocket, the old man took out a diamond signet ring, leaned down, and put it on the pinky of the wide-eyed corpse. Oddly, it fit, and that angered the old man. He sneered and then threw the corpse's arm back atop its body.

"I carry your bags no more, Sam Goren. No more," the old man said to the eyes that looked into nothing.

The old man chuckled. It was a perfect sight. Sam Goren was dead and gone from the old man's life forever.

"Hans," the old man said, "finish him. I vant no remnants of de bastard."

From inside the corpse's bag, the young man pulled out a wooden four-by-four post and began.

The old man watched as the end of the post heaved onto the face of the dead with brutal force and bludgeoned it to a pulp, blood seeping from the fresh kill. Now for the teeth. Those that escaped Hans's post, he plucked out and pulverized on the floor, which mixed well with the dust. A smile came to the young man's lips as each tooth was ground into powder, and then he looked at the old man.

The old man smiled, for the bloodletting did the dead justice. He couldn't be more pleased.

"I've had enough of your prowling," the old man said to the corpse. "Enough. Now you're a shell of a man who can never take vhat's not yours again. Never again, Sam Goren. Never again. You'll no longer take from me, you bastard. You're finally vhere you need to be—out of my life. Dis was long overdue—thirty-seven years overdue."

With that, the old man spit on the kill without a second thought. He sneered. Seeing the mutilated face of Sam Goren was sweeter than any expectations he could have. There were no words to describe the old man's enthusiasm.

"Set de charge. I vant no fingerprints or any udder problems," the old man barked as he turned and shuffled to the elevator.

The young man pulled a stick of C-4 from inside the bag that had held the corpse. The explosive was wired with a mercury detonator, and the young man placed it close to the body while the old man entered the elevator and pushed the button for the first floor. The old man refused to get his hands dirty. That was for Hans. Hans would do his bidding. The old man was in the clear.

Soon the elevator hummed as it climbed to the top and then back to the bottom. Once it reached the bottom, Hans helped the old man across the street as fast as the old man could go. Hans egged him on against the hard rain. As they crossed the street, they ran past Sam Goren's car and continued on. The plate read SG1. Halfway down the street sat an old Chevy. As they reached the old clunker, Hans opened the passenger-side door and helped the old man inside. Then he closed the door and ran to the driver's side.

"Let's go," the old man said, and they drove away from the dead district, as well as the dead Sam Goren.

From the glove box, the old man took out a signaling device. He pulled the antenna to its fullest extent and then pressed the red button. Within a millisecond, the sound of a massive explosion blew through the warehouse district. A ball of fire followed that turned night into day.

"Ve must hurry. Dhey're vaiting," the old man said. The district had flames of life again—his life, his flames.

They turned a corner and were gone.

After a good twenty miles, they arrived at a forgotten airstrip north of the city. There, a private jet was idling, ready for passengers. Hans stopped the car, jumped out, and ran around the car to aid the old man's exit and got him to the plane, but the old man shoved Hans away. He needed no help. As the old man walked to the plane, Hans left another stick of C-4 with the same detonator on the passenger's seat. With haste, Hans hurried to the old man, who'd taken the stairs of the jet. The door closed as the old man took his seat.

"You know vhat to do, Hans," the old man said and patted the young man on the arm.

Hans nodded, went to the front of the plane, and gazed upon the Chevy through the jet's window. As soon as the plane was up and in flight and the Chevy was the size of a peanut, he took another signaling device from his pocket. He pulled up the antenna and pushed the red button. From their altitude, Hans saw a flash of light explode into the night, almost like a firecracker with muscle. He went to the old man and stood as if waiting for his puppy treat for doing well.

The old man smiled at him and then leaned back into his chair with closed eyes.

It was done.

Chapter Two

"**S**am Goren," the newspaper reported, "was a successful jeweler in the diamond industry and a loving father, survived by his daughter, Danielle."

She tossed the obituary onto her loveseat with little regard. "Loving father my ass," she retorted, quite satisfied the s.o.b. was dead, and zipped up her leather skirt. Danielle didn't need to read the whole piece. What she'd seen was enough.

She would have liked to have shaken the killer's hand, but she didn't want to seem over the top. Instead, she stepped to her bed and, from under her pillow, pulled out a Walther PPK, a nice pistol without a lot of kick. "With Sam gone, I won't be needing you anymore. Good bye, ol' friend."

She softly smiled at the gun and then dropped it into her nightstand drawer. She grabbed her diamond signet ring from the top and put it on.

After she walked to her floor-length mirror to give herself a once over, Danielle donned her heels and grabbed her matching blazer.

"No more Sam. I don't believe it." She shook her head. "So what's wrong with this picture?" she murmured and then headed for the door without another thought—at least for now.

Sam was killed a month before; it took that long to identify the body. It was next to impossible except for his signet ring and car in the front of the building. DNA couldn't be used to identify the corpse, he was so crispy. They could only assume and let it go at that. Quite frankly, she could have cared less as long as the bastard was going in the ground. Danielle knew it was a horrid thing to say or even think, but she had to be honest. During that month, she hadn't even missed him. To her, he was in Europe like he had been so often for the past five years. It had only had been a week since the police told her, but she didn't care. During that month it was like a breath of fresh air—just like any other time the bastard was gone. Then she heard, "Danny," from the bottom of the staircase.

As she walked down the open stairway, she saw a portly woman at the bottom. It was Danielle's maid, but more importantly, her confidante, Beatrice "Bert" Arnold.

"Now Danny, if you can't look unhappy, at least fake it," Bert said.

"Of course …"

This was all a game to Danielle—just niceties. No one but Bert knew the *love* between her and her father; no one.

"Rafi flew all the way from Tel Aviv for the funeral," Bert mentioned.

"And you were expecting …? He's giving the damn eulogy. Criminy, I hope he doesn't carry on for hours."

Bert just pursed her lips. She knew there was no love lost between Danielle and Rafi. It was too bad; they would have made a good pair. But that was Bert's maternal side talking, and she knew it.

"Is the limo here yet?"

"I don't know." Bert went to the window in the large entry to look.

"Aren't they the ones who ring the doorbell?"

Just as Danielle asked, the bell rang.

"Now, Danny, try to be good," Bert said, shaking her finger.

"Going to the funeral is being good. Don't push it."

Bert rolled her eyes, grabbed her coat, and opened the door. "We'll be with you in a moment," she told the driver.

The driver tipped his hat and walked back to the limo.

Danielle walked out into the fresh air. The November leaves had all but gone, and the trees seemed so frail and sad, all but the oaks. They looked like arthritic fingers looking for a handout. She snickered. Great Neck, New York, never looked so uninviting. From her window in the limo, she gazed at the estates of large lawns and small castles. With an overcast sky, everything looked so dead. Her snicker widened. Sam was dead—as dead as the weather. She'd rather be at the office than dealing with this crap, but the one light in her life at that moment was that Sam was going in the ground. That seemed to brighten the dreariest of days.

Dear God, she thought, *if people only knew.* A bittersweet smile came to her face as she lit a cigarette and thought of Sam.

* * *

Danielle could hear the pandemonium at the funeral home. Everybody and their brother seemed to want to say good-bye to the late, great Sam Goren. He was quite the philanthropist good guy when needed. Since Danielle was in the family room off to the side of the main receiving room with Bert, Danielle couldn't see everyone there, except for Rafi Cardinel. Out of respect, she'd called him with the news about Sam's death on the night she found out. It was righteous indignation on Danielle's part. Sam and Rafi had been close for eighteen years or so. Sam had helped Rafi build up his diamond business in Israel. Rafi was the son Sam never had.

Danielle had her own father-daughter relationship with Abe Stern. He'd taken her under his wing at around the same time Sam had Rafi. Sam and Danielle had no relationship except for their hatred. Both were guilty of that—but there was always a reason for all emotions, no matter how misplaced. Out of the blue, Sam had given Danielle free reign over the business five years before, and she ran with it. Danielle was more than qualified and did very well. Abe was always there to help if needed since he was in the same business, but Sam never was. She was bold and daring, and no one could do what she'd done with the business. Her quotas were far reaching.

Danielle had listened to the BS about Sam from the rabbi and now the eulogy from Rafi. Danielle cringed as she listened to his acclaim of Sam. It was truly sickening.

"Too bad I couldn't have given the eulogy," Danielle said to Bert.

"Danny, the man is dead."

"See, every cloud does have a silver lining."

"Danny ..."

"How long is this going to take?"

"Why? You planning on going somewhere?"

"I'd like to."

Bert just sighed in resignation. She knew all about Sam and Danielle's relationship. She was front and center and the only one who knew about it; not even Rafi knew. Danielle was all alone in that regard.

At the cemetery, the services were shorter than at the funeral home. To Danielle it was a blessing, but more than that, it gave her a chance to see who was there and who wasn't. That prodded her to narrow her eyes through her sunglasses. It was strange that Abe wasn't there. Abe didn't like Sam, but Danielle figured he'd be there just to make sure the bastard was really dead. So where was he?

The consolation meal was held at Danielle's house. Caterers ran in and out of the kitchen and into the dining room with their goodies for the dog and pony show. Cars lined the driveway and spilled out into the street. Danielle thought it was a fucking circus. Hell, even the clowns were all present and accounted for. As Danielle and Bert peeked into the dining room, Bert grabbed Danielle's arm and said, "Now, Danny, be good."

"This isn't a day to be good. It's a day to be careful."

And speaking of all the clowns, all of Sam's cohorts were in the dining room. In the corner was the largest of the clowns, Baron Edmond DeViamond. He was a pompous prick and Sam's best buddy. He put his monocle to his eye and gave Danielle a nod. A true sleaze bucket from way back, he was in the diamond industry as well. It was his family business. Danielle just tipped her head, crossed her arms, and leaned a shoulder against the doorframe. She figured that was all he deserved.

Bert stood behind Danielle and looked over her shoulder into the dining room. "A lot of people," she commented.

"Sam was always quite the personality when in motion," Danielle replied. "And all this for Sam. Good Lord."

"The baron looks distraught," Bert noted.

"About as distraught as a plague salesman."

"Danny, the man flew all the way from Amsterdam to be here."

"Funny, his arms don't look tired, and as far as Amsterdam goes, it's deductible."

"Danny ..."

Danielle next looked at a waif of a woman standing next to the baron—Lydia Small. She had been Sam's secretary for over twenty years. Danielle had always wondered about that woman. How could she be with Sam for that long?

"Lydia looks good," Bert mentioned.

"Yeah, for someone who'd been screwin' Sam."

"Danny ..." Bert poked Danielle in the ribs.

"Look, I'm just happy Boris is working out for me."

"As happy as Sam was with Lydia?"

That voice. Danielle didn't need to turn. She didn't need to look but did and placed a gracious smile on her lips without looking too artificial.

"Well, Cardinel. It's nice to see you here."

"I could say the same thing to you, Danielle."

Danielle's graciousness dropped like the mercury on a cold day. "Oooh, that hurt. I didn't think we were going to get nasty until the bonus round."

Bert just looked down, not knowing what to say. She knew their history as well.

"Excuse me, Cardinel. There's a lot of people here I don't want to see," Danielle said and then walked away.

* * *

In her library, Danielle fell back against the double doors as if to keep the ills of the world out or possibly to a dull roar. She admitted she'd been sarcastic, droll, and dry, but Cardinel always did bring out the best in her.

Rafi Cardinel, she thought. Sam's son or the son of Sam might be more appropriate. And what was she to Sam—chopped liver? Quite frankly, yes. Was she jealous of Sam's and Rafi's relationship? No.

She knew what Sam was capable of because she'd been at the other end of the stick. (She knew the Jekyll from the Hyde.) Sam's death was merely a tit-for-tat.

She had Abe, yet he wasn't at the funeral, which was more than odd. As she'd thought before, he should have been at the funeral, if nothing else but to ease her pains—like there were any. That's why Danielle went to the funeral—not out of necessity, though it did look good on her part. But Rafi … She knew she sounded like she'd been vaccinated with a phonograph needle, but Rafi *was* the son Sam never had. But then, Rafi had been manipulated by the master. She didn't mean to make it sound as if Sam didn't really care about Rafi, because he sincerely did. She knew that for a fact.

Rafi Cardinel had been a thorn in her side for over eighteen years, yet he was a man to be reckoned with, though she'd rather not. He was intelligent, forthright, and a damn good person. Sam had helped Rafi turn his small diamond business into an empire unto itself. It wasn't that Danielle didn't like Rafi because she did. She just couldn't understand how an intelligent man like Rafi Cardinel could fall for Sam. She couldn't down him for it. Sam's eloquent pandering could bullshit anyone … anyone but her. Shrewd, cunning, and far from being naïve, Sam was the kind of man who'd stab you in the back while paying for the dinner he'd just served you, and all with a smile.

Danielle walked to her desk and pulled out the middle drawer. There, in plain sight, was Sam's half-melted ring. The initials were barely legible, but the one-carat diamond was still housed in the ring. It didn't mean a damn thing to her. She felt no emotions as she picked it up and looked at it—not one damn emotion except maybe the one she shouldn't: relief. Either way, she wouldn't give it much more thought.

Then she thought of her mother. Sam had killed her with emotional corruption. She'd lost her mind, her sense of self, and her dignity. Danielle didn't know the exact circumstances, but Bert told her what she could—or maybe what she could for Danielle. Sam broke her mother down like a bridge of toothpicks in a soft windstorm, one stick at a time, consistently and methodically. Her mother had no support system in her life. She was one of those ladies who kept family matters private, where they should be. In other words, she was alone and most likely feared not only for her life but also for Danielle's. Danielle's mother had gotten the wrong end of the stick as well, just worse. Danielle remembered very little of her mother. It would be difficult at age four, but maybe it was just enough.

As Danielle thought more about Sam's death, the more it made no sense. Sam would be too cunning to have put himself in that sort of position. It just didn't make any sense. As she thought before, something was wrong with this picture, but she didn't have the time or inclination to even think about it at that moment. With all the people in the house, she couldn't make the time, but something wasn't right in little Great Neck. She'd deal with it later when all the guests had left and she had her house back to herself.

Then the doors opened. It was Bert.

"People are leaving."

"Thank God for small favors. Does that mean I have to push them out myself?"

"It would look good on your part, Danny."

She sauntered to the door. "Fine."

Danielle did what she should.

Chapter Three

The guests were gone, and the house lay quiet.

In the library, Danielle had Stan Getz playing mellow jazz as she looked at Sam's signet ring. She sat behind her large mahogany desk, yet it still didn't seem right to her. *How could Sam put himself in a position to be murdered?* she asked herself again. It just didn't seem kosher. She dropped his ring on the desktop. She stood and went to the floor-to-ceiling windows to watch the night's rain and think.

Bert walked in and took a seat in one of the high–backed chairs in front of the desk. Danielle crossed her arms and seemed to ignore her.

It was a large room—almost as large as a pharaoh's tomb—but the house itself was as big as the pharaoh's temple.

"A lot of people were at the funeral," Bert finally said.

"Just goes to show you can fool most of the people most of the time."

"Danny, the man is dead."

"See, there is a God." After a moment, Danielle shook her head and then said, "I suppose I shouldn't have said that." She turned her head and looked at Bert from over her shoulder. "So why don't I believe in it?"

Bert didn't comment. She just sighed and left well enough alone. She walked to the bar cart to pour a brandy for Danielle. She brought it to her and said, "Here. You look like you could use one."

Danielle softly smiled at Bert, took the snifter, and said, "Thanks, Bert. You're my hero for the day."

"You did well at the funeral. I know how hard it must have been for you," Bert said.

"Speaking of which, did you see Abe Stern today?" Danielle turned back to look out at the rain.

"No. Were you expecting him to be there?"

"As a matter of fact, I was. He should have been there. I can't understand why he wasn't."

"It was nice of Rafi to give the eulogy."

"It was nice of Rafi not to carry on."

"Anyway, I thought it was a nice service."

"As I said, Sam's in the ground. It was a nice service."

Bert sighed to herself as Danielle took a large gulp of her brandy, which was fitting for the circumstances.

"Would you like another, Danny?" Bert asked, seeing that the snifter was three-fourths gone.

"Damn," Danielle hissed under her breath. "No, Bert, I think I'll have the decanter."

Bert walked to the windows to look for herself. "A visitor at this hour?"

"No, the grievance committee."

"It looks like Rafi."

"Same difference."

"I'll let him in," Bert said as she turned to answer the door.

"Why? He's got a damn key."

Bert stopped in the doorway, turned, and said, "I like Rafi, Danny. He's the kind of man you don't forget."

"Like the IRS?"

Bert just sighed and disappeared from the library to answer the door.

A groan burrowed from under Danielle's breath. This was not what she needed—not tonight. She walked back to her desk just to make sure there'd be distance between the two of them. She took a cigarette from its holder and lit it with its matching lighter that sat next to her Seiko. Inhaling deeply, she released it with a sigh. She could tell him she was doing paperwork, but either way it was a losing proposition. He'd still be there.

"Why tonight?" she asked out of frustration. "Hell, why any night?"

Soon she heard voices—Bert's and Rafi's. She looked at her empty snifter and wished she did have the decanter. She just placed the empty on her desk.

Rafi stood in the doorway of the library for a moment. Danielle wanted to say he looked like a wet spaniel, but his olive complexion and dark hair and mustache wouldn't let her. The one thing she could sense was that he came in peace. That pissed her off.

"So, Cardinel, did you come back for the bonus round or to lick your wounds?"

"Hello to you too, Danielle."

"Have a seat, Cardinel. Tell Bert your pleasure."

"A brandy will be fine, thank you, Bert," he said and took a seat across from Danielle.

"Home to stay or just wanting to ruin what's left of a perfectly rotten day?" Danielle took another drag of her cigarette.

Rafi just rolled his eyes. He watched Danielle push her sweatshirt sleeves to her elbows. "I wanted to apologize for that remark I made earlier," he said as he leaned back in his chair.

"Please don't. God forbid our relationship should become civil."

Bert placed two snifters of brandy on the desk and took Danielle's used one.

"Thank you, Bert," Danielle said.

"Well, I'll leave you two alone," Bert said and then turned and walked out, closing the doors behind her.

Rafi reached for his brandy and then settled himself in his chair.

Danielle couldn't have cared less one way or the other that he was even there. It didn't take long for him to return. She wondered why he would, except for a free bed. An apology wasn't what she had in mind, but it made for a good story. Danielle picked up Sam's ring from atop the desk and tossed it to him.

"Take it," Danielle said and then took a drink of her brandy.

Rafi picked it up and examined it with a furrowed brow. Then he looked at Danielle. "This was Sam's."

"You're quick tonight, Cardinel."

"Why did you toss it to me?"

"You're his favorite son. You should have it."

"Danielle, I can't take this. You're his daughter. You should have it."

"Ah, but Daddy loved you best."

Her tone was quasi-facetious but she meant it. The comment confused him as his features slightly skewed.

"Danielle," Rafi began with a softer voice, "your father loved you a great deal.

Danielle wanted to laugh but didn't have the energy. "No he didn't." She stood and carried her brandy to the sofa before the burning fire. "By the way, my condolences to you. You were just lucky he only allowed you to see his good side."

Rafi turned his body to look her way from around the chair. "Why do you say that?"

"Because it's true. You didn't know Sam the way I knew Sam. Let's just leave it at that."

Rafi stood and walked to the back of the sofa. He looked at Danielle through the mirror above the fire's mantel and said, "Maybe it was you who didn't know him."

Danielle turned to look up at him and said, "I'm the one who lived with the man. Doesn't my vote count?"

"I didn't know we were keeping score." Rafi walked around the sofa and took a seat in one of the chairs that sat to the side.

"With you, we're always keeping score. That's our relationship, Cardinel. It'll never change."

"Are you jealous of Sam's and my relationship?"

"No. I'm just glad you two got along so well. It's nice to know he had the capability of being a father to someone."

"Maybe you were too close to the situation."

"Oh, right, Cardinal. I should have lived in Tel Aviv and had a relationship with him from afar like you did."

Danielle rolled her eyes and took a large swig of her brandy. Then she flicked her cigarette into the fire. She'd like to tell Rafi about the real Sam Goren, but she didn't want to burst his bubble. Hell, he'd never believe it anyway.

"By the way, thank you for calling me personally about Sam. I do appreciate it," Rafi said, interrupting her thoughts.

"Contrary to popular belief, Cardinal, I'm not completely heartless."

"I never said you were," Rafi said defensively. He wore a face fostered by years of trying to see through her facade.

Danielle took another sip of her brandy as she looked at him from over the rim of her glass. When she finished with that sip, she said, "The reading of the will is tomorrow at nine a.m."

"Yes, I know. I was notified by Sam's lawyer."

"It should prove to be a good time."

"Why? Because I was told?"

Danielle refused to answer. She changed the subject and said, "Your room is ready for you. Bert's probably turning down your bed as we speak."

"Personally, I thought you might want to be alone. I'm sure it was a hectic day for you."

"It makes no difference to me, Cardinal. Whenever you're in New York you stay here, so what's the difference? But thanks for the thought."

"To be honest, Danielle, I don't know why I was even asked to hear the will. Frankly, I can't see anything Sam would leave me."

Danielle sat up, leaned toward Rafi, and said, "You're here for a reason, Cardinal. Of *that* I can assure you."

Rafi stared at her quizzically and took a sip of his brandy. "What's in the will, Danielle? If you know something, it would be a help."

Danielle stretched her arms across the back of the sofa and answered, "There will be surprises. That, I can guarantee."

"Danielle, I sincerely don't have any idea what you're talking about."

"Don't worry. You'll know it when it happens, but don't say I didn't warn you. In other words, Cardinal, expect the unexpected. This is the real Sam Goren we're talking about now. My advice to you is to keep that in mind."

Rafi took a sip of brandy and then said, "What is it that Sam would leave me, Danielle? Tell me."

"I haven't the faintest, but you've been asked here for a reason. Sam's not done yet."

"Done with what?"

"Honestly, I don't know, but as I said, you're here for a reason."

The sudden ring of the telephone interrupted their conversation, such as it was. Danielle didn't move but stayed quiet. Sipping on her brandy, she knew Bert would get it and fend off any sympathizers.

Suddenly, Bert burst through the doors. "Danny, it's Boris. You'd better talk to him."

Both Danielle and Rafi furrowed their brows as Danielle jumped over the back of the sofa and ran to pick up her phone on the desk. Danielle listened; Rafi watched.

"How?" Danielle asked. She listened on and then said, "I'm on my way. Don't do anything until I get there, and you and Marvin keep quiet. Absolutely no cops! Do you understand?" She waited for an answer and then replied, "Good," and slammed down the receiver.

"Cardinal, our visit must end. I'm out of here," Danielle said and headed for the door in a rush.

Rafi had never seen Danielle in such a state. He followed her to the door, agitated. "Danielle, what is it?" he asked intently.

"Not now, Cardinal. I don't have time for you at this moment."

He grabbed her arm and swung her around. "Make the time! Now! What's wrong?"

She looked at his hand on her arm and then at him. "If you don't let go, I swear I'll beat you like a rented mule! I can handle this myself. You don't own Goren's yet."

"I don't care what I have or not," he said and gripped her arm tighter. "Now tell me what's wrong!"

"The Goren security stones are missing! Yeah know, the stones that secure my business! Happy!"

His brows lowered. "I'm coming with you."

"Fine. I suppose I could use a committee about now, but I'm driving."

"Fine," Cardinel mumbled.

"Let's go." Danielle grabbed her trench coat.

They ran out the door and through the rain to her Lotus Elite. Rafi had to make an effort to fall into the car since he was tall and had long legs. As they took off, Rafi's stomach jumped into his throat, and it wasn't because of Danielle's driving. He'd never seen her so distraught before. To him, she'd always been a cool, if not cold, customer. He'd never seen like this—anxiety ridden. It was stenciled across her forehead—*help!* He wished he knew what else was up, but he'd soon find out.

Chapter Four

Boris, Danielle's lanky red-headed secretary, met them at the door of Goren's. They walked through the waiting area, unlocked the second security door, and then walked down the long hall past the sales rooms and to her office at the back. There, Marvin, her head diamond cutter, was waiting.

"Marvin, what the hell happened?" Danielle demanded.

"Go look for yourself," Marvin said as he mopped his bald head with a handkerchief. "I was putting away some new cuts and saw that the stones were gone."

"Son of a bitch, they took the entire box!" She walked out of the vault and looked at Rafi. "If this gets out, I'll be out of business before lunch tomorrow."

"Who could have done this, Danielle?" Rafi asked.

"That's the thing, Cardinel. No one has that combo to the safe but me, Marvin, and ..." She put a hand to her forehead. "And Sam."

"It couldn't be Sam, Danielle," Rafi said. "He wouldn't steal from himself."

"Oh no? I've told you, you don't know Sam like I do. And stealing would be right up his alley."

"Why?"

"Like I said, Cardinel, he'd be stealing from me, not himself. I've had the business for over five years. He's stealing from me."

Danielle went to her desk, pulled out the top drawer, grabbed an open pack of cigarettes, and lit one. After she blew out a billow of smoke, she said to all, including Rafi, "Tell no one of this until I can figure out what the hell is going on."

Boris and Marvin nodded in agreement.

"Danielle, you can't keep up appearances like this."

"Watch me, Cardinel. Just keep your mouth shut as well."

Danielle paced back and forth, thinking of what to do, and then finally took a seat behind her desk. It served her well as she let her head fall to the back of the chair and took another drag of her cigarette. She lifted her head and said to the boys, "Go home. I'll handle this."

"Are you sure?" asked Marvin.

"Yes, I'll be fine, and so will the company. Sam never knew I had my own plans, thank God. I'm not out of the woods yet, but we'll make it. Just don't open your mouths. That includes you too, Cardinel."

"Danielle, you know me better than that," Rafi said.

"Maybe. Don't push it." She looked at Marvin and asked, "What are you doing here so late?"

"I was getting an order ready for tomorrow."

"And I had some notes to go over," Boris answered.

"Go home. You've done all you can. I'll see you in the morning."

The two men walked from her office and closed the door behind them.

After the two had left, Rafi said, "I know we've never seen eye to eye, but …"

"Not now, Cardinel," Danielle interrupted.

"Do you want me to drive you home? You're in no condition to drive."

"I've been robbed, Cardinel, not knocked up. But I'll let you. It'll give me time to think of what happened to my stones. They were the ten originals stones Sam used to open the business with. So who took them?"

Danielle had no answers for the stolen stones except Sam. But how could he have pinched them and when? It was obviously quite easy. The bastard still had his keys to the joint and could have made off with them at any time. But why now? Or why at all? This was a night she'd like to forget but couldn't. Her business depended on her and those stones. She put her cigarette out.

"Danielle, if there's anything—"

"Forget it," she interrupted again. "We'll know more tomorrow."

"Why do you say that?"

"It's the reading of the will, or have you forgotten?"

"How can that help?"

"Whether or not you know it, Cardinel, you're still a very large factor in this equation."

Rafi ignored the comment and asked, "Danielle, do you know who did this?"

She nodded yes but said, "No." She then stepped to the windows to look out over the city.

Rafi looked at her skeptically. "Danielle, do you know who could have done this? It couldn't be Sam. Why would he steal from his own company?"

"I already told you, he hasn't been involved with the company for over five years. But why indeed? I know who did this, but you'd never believe it even if it bit you on the ass, so just drop it. I'll be fine as long as it doesn't hit the streets."

"You seriously think it was Sam?"

She stayed quiet. She walked back to her desk, retrieved another cigarette, and lit it, the other one still smoldering in the ashtray.

Rafi tipped his head with a worried look. He didn't understand her feelings, but then again, he didn't expect to. He was used to the mystery.

Danielle knew who did this. She knew Rafi would just refuse to believe her. He had always had an inexplicable naiveté about Sam's character.

"So what are you going to do, Danielle?"

"There's nothing I can do. I'll just have to deal with it the best I can."

"Can you replace them?"

"Please, Cardinel. You know the answer to that one," Danielle said as she put her cigarette out. Then she said, "Let's go."

"I'll drive. Remember?"

"And I'll let you. Remember?" Danielle answered and tossed him the keys. "I feel like I've just been raped, but there's no back alley." She grabbed a smoke for the road and said, "Let's get the hell out of here. The ghosts are beginning to rear their ugly heads."

She walked to the safe, shut the large, heavy door, and spun the dial. They were gone.

* * *

There was silence between the two as they walked up the stairs at Danielle's home. As they hit the top of the stairs, Danielle said, "Good night, Cardinel. Sleep well."

"And you, too, Danielle. If—"

Danielle put her finger to his lips, and said, "It'll be all right."

She walked away and down the hall to her bedroom.

Never had Rafi heard her say good night to him, let alone sleep well. It made him wonder. It was out of character for her, and that bothered him. He knew she was between a rock and a hard place but left it alone, at least for the night. Tomorrow might be a better day, though he didn't know how.

Rafi went into his bedroom—the bedroom he always had when in New York. A small light on the bed stand Bert had obviously turned on put out a soft glow. He closed his door, took off his leather blazer, and put it on a chair. The small bag he'd brought with him was on the chest at the foot of his bed. Bert had already taken care of it for him as well. Taking a seat on the edge of his bed, he pulled out his cell, dialed a thirteen-digit number, and then waited for someone to pick up.

"Sir, it's Rafi." He listened to what was said and then answered back, "You were right. There was a break in at Goren's. The security stones were stolen."

Rafi listened to the voice on the other end and then said, "Yes sir. I'll find out what I can. The reading of the will is tomorrow, and I was told to be there. Why I don't know, but I'll find out and report when I get home." Rafi listened to the rest of the conversation and again said, "Yes, sir," and then closed his cell.

Still dressed, he lay down to think of the day and the worse night. Soon the jet lag and exhausting problems he was involved with soon put him to sleep.

* * *

One small lamp was on in Danielle's room as she stood by the window and looked out into the night. Sleep hadn't found her, but she never expected it to. Instead she found only aggravation, mistrust, and fear, but it was the fear that upset her the most. She knew who took her diamonds, but she couldn't prove it; he was dead. She could have told Rafi, but he wouldn't believe her, yet it was the only explanation she could find.

It had to have been Sam, but when did he do it? How did he do it? But most importantly, why did he do it? Was it to put her in a bad situation? Probably. Putting her in a bad situation was his way of playing with her and all from the grave. It was his ammunition. He might have given her Goren's to run for the past five years, but it wasn't out of the goodness of his heart. Sam had been planning this during that time. She just wished she knew why.

"Ah, hell," she uttered. She didn't know how she was going to get herself, and the company, out of this one.

"Bastard," she exclaimed under her breath.

She walked to her bedside table and lit a cigarette. Then she took a seat on the edge of her bed to think. She thought until she couldn't think anymore and didn't even want to. Tomorrow, when the will was read, she'd know what was true and what was not. Somehow, she felt all questions would be answered with the will.

Danielle put out her cigarette, turned off the light, and laid down, but sleep was far from her. Irritated, she got up, walked down the stairs, and headed for the library. She went directly to the bar cart and poured herself a brandy. Then she took a seat behind her desk. The situation was dire. Around three in the morning, her head was on the desktop with her arms to either side. Sleep finally found her.

Chapter Five

Rafi stood in the doorway of the library watching Danielle slumber. He knew she must be drained, not only from the funeral but also from the night before. Oddly, he thought she looked so innocent with her head and arms sprawled across the desk, her long, auburn hair strewn everywhere. Rafi empathized with her. A lot had happened within such a short period of time. He could only wonder how she was holding up. It made him wonder how he would have felt after last night's surprise.

Rafi looked at his watch. It was almost time for Sam's lawyer, Fred Shapiro, to read the will. Bert had told Rafi to wake Danielle up as Bert readied the coffee for everyone. He was almost afraid to, but …

He walked across the Persian carpets to her desk. "Danielle," he said softly, "it's time to wake up."

A murmur grew from the back of her throat as she slowly pulled herself up and threw her long waves of hair from her face. She looked at Rafi, somewhat startled, and then grasped her composure, something she found necessary to her soul.

"Sleep well, Cardinel?" Danielle asked through a yawn.

"I think the question should be how did you sleep?"

"Like shit." She was honest to a fault.

Danielle picked up a cigarette from its holder and lit it with the lighter. It was like a shot in the arm to her. That day, even her lungs needed to be fed.

Rafi walked to the windows and put his hands in his pockets. To Danielle, that act made her think he was hiding something from her either emotionally or logically.

"What's the weather like today?" she asked.

"Cloudy," was all he said. Then he remarked, "I know there's nothing in the will for me, Danielle. Maybe Sam wanted a new pair of eyes. That's all."

"Don't be so sure. I told you, you are here for a reason, and it's not to be a witness."

Rafi turned his head and peered at her from over his shoulder. She could see he was becoming unnerved. She made him suspicious, and she knew it. She could see it. Hell, she could feel it.

Curiously, he turned and looked back out the windows.

The sound of tinkling china took their attention looked toward the door. Bert walked in with a silver tray of coffee with creamer and sugar, three cups, and saucers. She placed them on the coffee table that sat between the fireplace and sofa.

"Coffee, Rafi?" she asked.

"Thanks, Bert."

"The pot for you, Danielle?"

"You read my mind, Bert."

Bert poured two cups of coffee and took one to Danielle and the other to Rafi.

Danielle greedily drank her coffee as if it were her saving grace, and it was. Looking at Rafi, she could see a bit of empathy began to grow from him. It was written on his face. As she drank her Coffee, for the first time in her life. She could see he felt sorry for her. That pissed her off. Did bad come in threes or was it just BS? If so, as Danielle would say, it was in the will. What if there was? How would she take it? But more than that, how would Rafi take it? Danielle had been strong, but was there a surprise? For her sake, she hoped not. Enough was enough.

Bert walked to the windows next to Rafi and saw a tall man with a silver briefcase and wool topcoat come up the front walkway. "Shapiro's here," she announced.

"Oh, goody," Danielle cynically said. "Now the party is complete. Stick around, Cardinel, the fun is just beginning," Danielle added and then took a large drag of her cigarette.

"Aren't you ever serious?" Cardinel replied.

"I was."

Through her cynicism lay the truth, and he knew it. He knew her all too well.

"I'll get the door," Bert said, but as she reached the library's door, Fred Shapiro stood motionless in his five thousand–dollar suit with Halliburton briefcase and three long strands of hair combed back.

"Don't you ever knock?" Danielle asked as Rafi stepped to the desk.

"And a fine good morning to you too, Danielle," the gaunt man replied. "The door was open, and I didn't think you'd mind since I am reading your father's will."

"I mind."

Damn, if that man didn't remind Danielle of Mr. Burns on *The Simpsons,* but Shapiro was only seventy-two.

Rafi and Shapiro shook hands and exchanged niceties, as expected. "Rafi, it's good to see you," Shapiro said and then looked at Bert. "And it's good to see you too, Bert."

She thanked him and then asked, "Would you like some coffee, Mr. Shapiro?"

"No thank you, Bert. This won't take long," he said with a smile, which Danielle had always maintained looked like the grill work on a fifty-seven Buick.

Shapiro placed his briefcase on her desktop, opened it, and took out a long legal document. From his inside breast pocket, he brought out a pair of half specs and placed them on his beak. He looked at each person in the room and then said, "Are we ready?"

"Thrilled, Shapiro. Now, start. Cardinel has a plane to catch by noon, and I want him on it." Danielle put her cigarette out as if to punctuate her statement but immediately lit another.

Shapiro dropped his smile and became all business. "Fine. If that's the way you want it, Danielle, that's what you'll get." He cleared his throat, looked at the document, and began. "I, Sam Goren, being of sound mind and …"

"Today, Shapiro," Danielle egged the man.

He looked at her sternly and said, "Danielle, you inherit the house, the property, and all that pertains to it." He pulled out his smile for her again. "Enjoy paying your taxes."

"With what?" Danielle ashed her cigarette.

"A job."

Here it comes, Danielle thought and inwardly groaned.

"Which is?"

Shapiro referred back to the document. "You, Danielle, will continue to run Goren's on a day-to-day basis, with Rafi Cardinel as chief CEO, having all final say over the business in all aspects." Shapiro looked at Rafi and said, "Congratulations, Mr. Cardinel. I couldn't have chosen a better man myself."

"I can," Danielle said flatly. She felt like she'd been violated, with no one to blame.

"No! This cannot be!" Rafi's tone was shocked. "Danielle should have Goren's, not me!" his rant continued. He looked at Danielle and exclaimed, "Danielle, do something!"

Shapiro looked at him and said, "I'm sorry, Rafi, but those are the stipulations of the will. Danielle can do nothing."

Rafi looked at her and said, "Danielle …"

Danielle stood as she put her cigarette out, walked to the doorway, turned, and said to all, "I've been through this too many times before. It bores me." She looked at Rafi and reminded him, "Didn't I say there'd be surprises?"

With dignity, she turned and disappeared to the staircase and continued to her room. She'd had it with this vulgarity. She was completely and utterly finished.

As she climbed the stairs, she thought, *Sam's fucking me from the grave. Bravo, Sam. Bravo.*

* * *

Rafi stood by Danielle's open bedroom doorway, watching her sit on her love seat in front of her bedroom's fireplace where a quiet fire burned—much softer than Danielle's disposition. At least that's what Rafi saw and felt. He'd never seen her cave in without a fight. He didn't know what to say. He was afraid his tongue would trip over his shoes. But she was right. He was there for a reason. *What else does Danielle know?* he wondered. Yet by the same token, he couldn't help but feel for her. It's not every day you have your company ripped out from under you and your mortal enemy pick it up. But Sam never did anything without a reason. Ravi knew that, and she did try to tell him.

"Danielle?"

"What do you need, Cardinal?" she asked, her attentions on the flames. Then she took a deep drag of her cigarette.

"Danielle, I don't know what to say."

"There's nothing to say. I'm working for you now." She turned and looked at him from over her shoulder. "I trust you. Just don't fuck up."

"You know I'll have to see your quarterlies."

"Oh, spare me, Cardinal. I've been running Goren's longer than you. You, as far as I'm concerned, are on a need-to-know basis. Take it or leave it."

"But I wouldn't be doing my job as your father asked."

"My father was an ass. You'll keep out of my way, business will carry on as usual, and everyone in fairy land will be happy."

There was silence from Rafi. He knew this wasn't the time to get into it. He'd wait until the time was right. When that was, he didn't know.

Rafi looked deep into her eyes. There was nothing more he could say. He believed in Sam and would do as he was asked. But at the same time, he realized how devastating this must feel to Danielle. Therefore, the only thing he could say was, "Good-bye, Danielle."

"Good-bye, Cardinal."

"We'll talk later."

"No we won't. Have a nice flight."

Danielle turned her attentions back to the fire, and Rafi turned and left.

* * *

Now alone, Danielle felt the need to move and thus stood, flicked her cigarette into the fire, and walked into her sitting room. *Criminy, Cardinel's gullible,* she thought as she shook her head. But then, he wouldn't know the truth if he was given an embossed invitation. She tried to warn him, but he was definitely Daddy's little boy. She just didn't expect him to take it so damn seriously. Her mistake; she should have known better. Now she had to answer to him. That she didn't need. It was a waste of valuable time and energy. But she'd play the game until he grew weary. She just hoped that wouldn't take too long. Danielle was already weary, and the fun had just started.

Danielle rolled her eyes. What else could she do at that point? She walked back into her bedroom to take a quick shower and change. She could hear her office calling, or was it Cardinel's office?

Chapter Six

A man walked toward the Diamond Center on Roken Street in Amsterdam. There were the usual curb-to-curb pedestrians and morning traffic cluster fuck. Honking horns and serums were the happening thing. The man was a perfect imitation of a deflated Twinkie with a bowler hat propped on his head. A briefcase was handcuffed to his wrist.

From across the street, British agent Thomas Hensley watched the man closely. "Package in sight," he said as he tipped his head toward his coat's lapel where a small microphone was attached.

The bowler continued on as briskly as the morning rush would allow.

Fifteen meters behind the bowler, another agent, Brit Spencer, kept pace. He too kept a vulture's eye on the man. Then he tipped his head into his lapel and said, "Package continuing."

From inside an empty third-floor apartment, Major David Nibbons peered out over Roken from the window through binoculars. He was plain clothed and the nervous type. He was tall and had that British military air about him. He wanted nothing more than for this mission to succeed.

At a desk, sitting in front of a radio, was a young man wearing headphones. The radio and desk were the only furnishings in the apartment.

"The package is in sight," the young man announced.

"Good," barked Nibbons. "Let's now hope it goes how we bloody well planned."

Nibbons began to pace the floor, leaving footprints in the dust. "This courier has to make it." He looked at the young man. "Tell them to stay close and work into his perimeter."

"Yes, sir," replied William Gosh as he then reported to the two agents.

Dodging the traffic like a matador, Hensley joined his partner, Spencer. The two looked above heads as they clawed their way through the pedestrians as fast as humanly possible. But suddenly, there was no sign of the bowler. It was as if he'd disappeared into an abyss. Soon they came upon an alley. Hensley looked down the narrow strip between buildings and stopped dead. Hensley grabbed Spencer and jerked him to look. Halfway down was a man laying on the cement as a curious cat sniffed at him. They looked at each other with apprehension and then hot footed it for the body, hoping like hell it was a drunk instead of their man. It had only been eight or so minutes.

Lying on his back with open eyes and a knife in his chest, was the Twinkie, his bowler not far from his head. Hensley let out a "shit" while Spencer just shook his head, lifting the dead man's arm. His hand had been *chopped* from his wrist, and the briefcase was gone.

Spencer leaned his head toward his lapel. "Package lost. Goods gone."

The young man in the apartment sighed and took off his headset. He turned and looked at the major. "Sir, the courier is dead with the diamonds gone."

Nibbons threw his binoculars to the floor, cracking a lens. "Damn it to bloody hell! We're no better than Interpol!" he exclaimed, completely frustrated. "Call Tel Aviv."

The young man took out his secured cell and dialed.

Chapter Seven

A frigid wind blew through DeViamond as if he were a screen door. He pulled his collar up around his neck. A smile grew as he watched the private jet taxi its way toward him. It'd been a week since he'd seen his close friend, and he couldn't wait to hear the news.

The jet stopped; the door soon opened. The old man stepped to the plane's door, aided by the young man who'd taken his arm. But the seventy-five-year old jerked his arm from the younger man's hold. He'd do this alone.

The old man was stout and wearing a wool top coat, Fedora, and black gloves, though they didn't cover his French cuffs or diamond-studded cufflinks. He climbed down the stairs and then stopped at the bottom. He took in a deep breath of the cold air as if challenging the elements. With an open smile, he walked across the tarmac to DeViamond, his hand extended as Hans obediently followed behind like a well-trained dog.

DeViamond was pleased to see the old man. They'd been through so much together through so many years. With an outstretched hand, he walked to greet him. They'd known each other when they were in their early twenties. DeViamond remembered how a small group of diamond buyers sent their snot-nosed kids to learn the underbelly of DeVorhes, the diamond company with *the* diamonds. They controlled 82 percent of the diamonds in the world. The old man was the only one of all of them who actually worked for the company as a supervisor. That's where it all began. The old man and DeViamond started their friendship with five diamonds the old man had taken and given to DeViamond for *safekeeping*. Their relationship was then committed to stone, literally. But DeViamond didn't want to think of that now. He just gazed at his friend as he came closer.

They shook each other's hands with exuberance.

"Sasal, my friend," DeViamond replied. "How was your trip?"

"Uneventful, tank God," Sasal Gornsky answered. "And our layover in Brussels was nice."

"I'm happy to hear that, my friend."

DeViamond began to shuttle Sasal to a limousine waiting not far away, with Hans in tow. DeViamond thought the cold was unbearable. Sasal seemed to revel in it. He could take the cold and a lot more. The old man was slow but very sturdy.

"How are tings here?" Sasal asked.

"On schedule," DeViamond reported proudly. "Our assassins are on the streets as we speak and doing their jobs quite well. Amsterdam was hit yesterday."

"And Lydia?"

"In her place."

Sasal chuckled as he nodded. "Dat's my girl."

DeViamond and Sasal reached the limo. The obedient Hans opened the door for them, waited for the men to slide in, and then closed the door. Hans then ran to the front of the limo and took a seat by the driver. Sasal and DeViamond could now talk.

DeViamond settled in his seat as the warmth of the car immediately hit him but had to ask, "So, you really do care for Lydia, don't you?"

Sasal nonchalantly answered, "She plays her part vell. Dhat's vhat I care about."

DeViamond knowingly grinned as the limo left the small airstrip.

"Now, tell me about dhe funeral," Sasal said.

DeViamond pursed his lips and looked out the window at the Netherlands' countryside. "Danielle snubbed me," he said, quite taken aback.

"Vhat, you vere expecting open arms?"

DeViamond harrumphed and crossed his arms high upon his chest.

Sasal narrowed his gray eyes and pulled his lips to a savory sneer. "She got vhat she deserved. Don't you vorry about dhat. She'll be arguing vit Rafi for some time. It's all so perfect."

"How would you know that?" DeViamond asked as he looked at Sasal quizzically from over his shoulder.

Ignoring the question, he said, "I'm just glad to be rid of dhat Sam Goren once and for all. Now ve can step up our plans."

"Then all went well?"

Sasal looked at DeViamond with vengeful eyes. "Of course. All my plans go as expected. You yourself should know dhat by now." He slyly grinned at himself. "All vent accordingly. De police know nutting."

DeViamond smiled as he looked at his friend's profile. It was done. Sam Goren was dead. As far as they were concerned, nothing could hold them back now—nothing.

Chapter Eight

That morning, Rafi drove to work in his Autobianci through the hectic streets of Tel Aviv. It was worse than Paris. The drivers played dodge ball and fender bender quite well. Cursing in Arabic was a given, since there are no swear words in Hebrew. Following the lines on the street was like asking all Israelis to come to one opinion; it wasn't going to happen. But Rafi liked his little car, especially the excessive taxes he didn't have to pay on it, though it seemed ironic. As wealthy as he was, he was driving a piece of shit. Yet it served its purpose, getting him from point A to B, as well as giving him the freedom to come and go as he pleased. Sitting behind a desk at Cardinel Limited was not his only job.

He drove the car into the underground parking of his building, Shalom Towers. It was a modern building made of glass and steel, unlike those in Jerusalem in which everything had to be made from *Jerusalem stone.* Not far from the elevators, he found a parking spot. Then he grabbed his briefcase and exited his heated car. A man was already waiting by the metal doors. *Good,* Rafi thought. He wouldn't have to wait so long for the elevator to arrive.

The doors opened, the two stepped in, and each pressed their appropriate floors. The man was going to the fifth. Rafi was on the top.

Rafi stepped out of the elevator and entered his offices. The usual bustle was on the buzz. His secretary, Hadassah, jumped him as soon as he passed her desk. She held out a long box that was marked, "*Personal.*"

"This just came for you special delivery," she said as she looked at him from over her glasses.

His eyes narrowed as he took the package, thanked her, headed for his office, which had modernistic décor, and closed the door. He tossed his briefcase onto the leather couch while he turned the box back and forth, looking for a return address. There was none. With suspicion in his eyes, he proceeded to open it.

He picked up his letter opener and cracked all the seals. Inside he found, wrapped in paper, a long, black box. He took out the box and opened it. He instantly shut it as if he'd seen a ghost. Maybe he had. He called for his secretary over his intercom to come in. She promptly entered. Holding out the box, he told her to put it in the vault. Because the inflection of his voice and the expression on his face, she took the box and guarded it with her hands as if it contained the world's greatest secrets. Then she walked from the room.

Rafi reached for his phone and dialed. As he waited for an answer, he stood to look out his windows at the Mediterranean, which was a few blocks away. He slipped off his coat and tossed it onto one of the chairs that sat in front of his desk. There were a few brave souls still willing to try the cold, early December waters. Personally, he could think of a few other entertaining choices, and they had nothing to do with swimming in sixty or so degree waters. Finally, an answer.

"Sir, it's Rafi. We need to talk."

* * *

That afternoon, Rafi walked through the halls of the Mossad headquarters to Ezra Herzog's office. Herzog was the man in charge of Operation Judah and was Rafi's commanding officer. The door was open, but Rafi knocked on it anyway as he stood just inside.

Herzog looked up from his papers on his desk and then stood to shake Rafi's hand. A bombastic, short man of sixty years, he smiled, truly happy to see Rafi, and his brown eyes twinkled as proof. He wore a short-sleeved shirt. Summer or winter, it was always short-sleeved shirts. However, through his grace and smiles lay the heart of a driven man—and he expected nothing less from his agents.

"Sir," Rafi said, shaking his hand briefly.

"Rafi, tell me what's bothering you," Herzog said as he crossed his arms atop his belly.

"It's that noticeable?"

"Yes, but this is different. It has to do with the diamond business, doesn't it?"

"You're right. That night I was there the Goren security stones were stolen. But today, I received a package. They're the Goren stones."

With dropped brows, Herzog said, "How do you know they're them?"

"Because I was the one who cut them. I had my best cutters on it. It was over ten years ago, but I know those stones."

"Who would steal the stones and then turn around and send them to you?"

"I don't have an answer, unless Sam did before he was murdered."

Herzog turned for his desk with one hand to his brow, thinking, analyzing, and ripping apart any other options there might be.

"Danielle thinks it's Sam somehow," Rafi said.

"But he's dead."

"That's why I don't understand any of this—my being the CEO of Goren's, the stones being sent to me. Someone went to a lot of trouble."

"What's Danielle's take?"

"I don't know."

The commander took his seat behind his desk and then looked at Rafi right in the eyes. "Get her here. She knows more than she's letting on, and I want to know what it is."

"How?"

"That's up to you, Captain. You're in charge of her. Take charge. It's time. I want her here within the week."

"But sir—"

"Keep me informed, Captain, and that's an order," he interrupted.

"Yes, sir."

And that was that.

Rafi stepped out of the office, and down the hall. Then he stopped momentarily. He wondered how the hell he was going to lure Danielle to Israel. Guilt began to surface its lowly head, but he couldn't disobey a direct order. This affair was becoming too tenuous to fake anymore. He'd heard of the Amsterdam incident. He realized he just couldn't up and ask her to come; she'd probably tell him where to go and how to get there. The problem was that he only had a week. That didn't leave much time. He let out a curse from under his breath and moved on.

As he left the building, his mind was mulling through all the possibilities. Then he thought of it. It was slightly cheesy, but it might work.

* * *

Danielle sat behind her desk in her black leather skirt with matching waist-cut jacket. It was dressy enough for the office yet comfortable enough to maneuver in. The calculated mess on her desk was in fanned bunches—a demented method to Danielle's madness. As she looked at the papers, her mind began to drift back to a time she'd rather not remember.

It was her childhood. It was like watching a slow motion train wreck, as she battled with Sam on an everyday basis. She had no friends. She was too serious of a little girl for children's meaningless interests. There were no sleepovers, no one coming to the house. She was too embarrassed for them to know the truth of her home life.

Suddenly, a kind of sadness enveloped her. But those other girls all bored her. There was more to life than clothes, money, and good looks. Her teenage companions made her want to become a socialist; Danielle thought they were so superficial. She had other issues—much more than issues, like getting through another day with Sam.

She remembered Sam finally did buy her a horse when she was sixteen. He probably thought it would keep her out of his hair, but she was more than happy to oblige. She poured her love into that animal and became one of the nation's top junior jumpers for two years straight. His name was Bobbie. Bobbie was the only one who understood her and honestly cared about her. They made quite the team as well. But Sam never came to her competitions. That was left up to Bert and Abe.

She felt a thin smile pull her lips as she remembered them sitting in the grandstands and taking pictures of her and Bobbie with her trophies and ribbons. She truly loved that horse. She also truly loved Bert and Abe for backing her. They were her friends. They were always there for her—never Sam But, it was obvious that some memories were best forgotten … some.

Then she heard a faintly spoken, "Danny?"

Danielle shook the cobwebs and looked up. "Yes, Boris?" she replied to the young man standing in front of her desk. He was holding an invoice.

"I thought you needed to see this immediately."

She took the blue slip and examined it. After a quick moment, she balked as if she'd just been smacked up the side of her head with a two-by-four. It was from Cardinel Limited; her monthly statement.

"When did this come?" she asked, still looking at the figures.

"It just arrived."

"What's he trying to do to me?" she asked, mainly to herself. She looked at Boris. "Have you read this?"

He nodded. "That's why I thought you should see it."

She was shocked and looked back at the slip as if it'd been sprinkled with blood. A note was written at the bottom in Rafi's handwriting: "If you have any questions I'll be in my office late this week."

"Questions," Danielle retorted. "I've got a few questions like, may I have your head?"

"Maybe he made a mistake, Danny."

"Cardinel doesn't make mistakes," she said irritably. She said, "Put in a call to Cardinel. Put him through the second he's on line.

Something's wrong with this picture, and I think it's the frame. Two hundred percent above his normal price. Yeah … right."

"Got it, Danny," Boris said and hurried out of her office.

* * *

Danielle waited for Cardinel's call all day but never heard from him. That made her even more suspicious than she already was. That wasn't like him. *He wants something,* she thought, *and I'll be happy to reciprocate.*

She folded the blue slip, tucked it into her inside breast pocket, and called Boris to her office.

He opened the door and poked his head in. "Yes, Danny?"

"Book me on the next flight to Tel Aviv. I'm leaving," she announced, standing and gathering her things.

"On it."

Boris vanished as Danielle put the papers in her briefcase. About ten minutes later, Boris came back into her office. "I booked you on a flight that leaves tonight at eleven-thirty."

"Good," she said as she walked from her office. "Have Marvin close up shop. I'll call you when I get to Israel."

Boris nodded and then remarked, "Danny, this is a bad time to bring it up, but my top desk drawer still sometime sticks. I can only it out halfway, and that's on a good day."

"I promise to buy you a new one when I get back. I promise."

"Great!"

Danielle smiled and then started down the hall to leave as Boris called, "Have a nice flight."

Danielle merely waved her hand as she left.

* * *

Danielle had just enough time to get back to her house, change into a pair of leather pants, pack a few things, and leave again. Security was brutal, especially El Al's. They were notorious for their screenings, but they had to be. Threats were an hourly occurrence.

She zipped her bag, and with bag in hand, she headed out her room and down the stairs. Bert was waiting for her at the bottom.

"Now, remember, call me when you get there," Bert said in a motherly fashion.

"Promise. And have Boris pick up the Tahoe at Kennedy. I don't know how long I'll be gone."

"Will do."

"See yeah later."

Danielle was out the door.

* * *

A dark-headed man watched from a short distance as Danielle picked up her ticket at the El Al counter. He put a cell phone to his ear and said, "Parcel posted." Then he flipped his cell shut and followed Danielle onto the plane.

* * *

It was eight o'clock in the morning. Herzog was conducting a meeting in an almost-sterile conference room at Mossad headquarters. There was a blackboard on the wall with eight names on it. Sam Goren's was at the bottom. Maps of Israel and the Middle East were on the walls, and a rolled-up screen, for movies or slides, hung from chains at the front of the room.

Rafi sat at the long table surrounded by six other Israelis and one blond-headed Brit from MI5, Mathew Somner, their mole into DeVorhes. The other men were Erez N'Gar, Avi Abrams, Shlomo Wolf, Noshi Kolachi, Moshe Stein, and Yoseph Pearl. Each had his own area of expertise. From documents to explosives, they filled the bill. Their ages ranged. Most were young, in their early twenties. Shlomo was the exception at forty-five, as was Rafi. Shlomo was one of their weapons experts. Avi was the youngest and was the team's communications expert.

This was a joint effort between MI5 and the Mossad to stop this diamond fiasco. Even though DeVorhes was based in England, Israel just had as much at stake. Tel Aviv was a major diamond center, just as Antwerp and Amsterdam, not to mention New York. But it was the Mossad that had a reputation for *getting things done*. Therefore, Herzog was the coordinator with Nibbons's second in command. The men who sat at the table were the main team, the heart of the operation. Intelligence was coming in from everywhere, but initial plans were made here with these men.

"These are the men who have been murdered since last March," Herzog began, tapping on the board with the names on it. "Sam Goren was two months ago. Also, Goren's diamond collection was found stolen on the night of his funeral. The daughter, Danielle, believes she knows who did it, as reported by Rafi."

"Did she come out and say it?" asked Shlomo.

"No," Rafi answered, "but her mannerisms might as well have."

"Rafi has arranged for her to be here," Herzog continued. "She thinks it's because a grievance over billing from Rafi. I believe what she knows we need to know, which is why Rafi did this. We have conformation that she's on the plane now and will land a little after five tonight. Rafi …"

Rafi cleared his throat and then spoke. "I expect her to come to my office immediately after she checks into a hotel. She's mad and will want to see me as soon as possible." He looked at Herzog. "But I really don't see how she can help us." He was trying to keep her out of it.

Herzog could feel Rafi hedging and remarked, "Another courier was killed and the diamonds taken just three days ago in Amsterdam. From our intel, it sounds like this group won't be happy with just taking out couriers for much longer. I have a feeling they have bigger and better things in mind. They've got a hard on for DeVorhes, which hits everybody in the balls." He looked at Rafi. "I'll take what I can get from where I can." He turned his eyes back to the group. "We meet at Rafi's office at six tonight. Mathew, when is your flight?"

"This afternoon. I start working for DeVorhes tomorrow."

"Good. I want a weekly report from you personally."

Somner nodded. "Of course, sir."

"Remember, Rafi's at six. Dismissed."

✳ ✳ ✳

From the airport, Danielle took a Mercedes taxi to the Dan Hotel, but all the taxis in Israel were Mercedes—an ongoing peace offering from the German government.

Danielle checked in and had her bag taken to her room while she went to the bar. At that moment, jet lag was the furthest thing from her mind. She needed a brandy to take the edge off. Belting Cardinel right off the mark might seem a bit forward. She'd let him explain himself, and then she'd belt him.

Danielle looked at her watch. It was a little after 6:00 p.m. Darkness had already fallen. Cardinel said he'd be in his office late. That meant he'd be in his office until at least eight.

Danielle took a large dram of her brandy and swirled it in her mouth. The burning sensation made her wonder what he was up to, and she knew it wasn't to make points with her. She'd leave after her drink.

* * *

Rafi stood by the windows of his office, watching the lights of the city reflect off the Mediterranean and loathing this deception. But then again, she did know more than she was telling, and he wanted to know what it was as much as Herzog. The main team was by the leather couch, with Herzog playing ring master. The men talked amongst themselves as Herzog stepped to Rafi's side.

"It's been over an hour. You're sure she'll come?"

"She's mad at me. She'll come." Rafi looked back out the windows. "Believe me, she'll come."

The phone rang. Rafi stepped to his desk and answered. "Yes?"

"Parcel on delivery," he heard and then replaced the receiver.

Rafi looked at Herzog and said, "She's on her way up."

After hearing those precious words, a gleam came to Herzog's eyes. He clapped his hands to grab everyone's attention. "Places gentlemen," he ordered as he hurried to the light switch.

Herzog watched his men back away from the couch and next to the wall while Rafi took his place behind the desk. Herzog flicked off the lights and then joined his men. The only light left was Rafi's banker's light on his desk, which not only lit his desk but also encircled part of the floor. The scene was set. Now for the main character.

* * *

Danielle stepped off the elevator and to the front door of Cardinel Limited. She pressed what looked to be a doorbell. She immediately heard a buzz. Her eyes narrowed. At this hour, Cardinel would have asked who it was, she thought. Now she knew he was expecting her, but how?

She opened the door and walked in, letting the door close and self lock behind her. The heels of her boots echoed throughout the silent hall as she made her way to his office. When she arrived, Rafi's door was open, but she jerked to a stop at the doorway and looked the atmosphere over. She felt as if she'd stepped into a slasher movie and refused to go any farther. She then looked straight across the room. Rafi was sitting at his desk, full front and sober, looking straight at her with hands folded atop his desk.

Danielle remarked flatly, "Tell me I'm not in a bad Claude Rains movie."

"You're not in a bad Claude Rains movie."

Danielle walked to the front of his desk, stopped, and sailed the invoice onto his desk. "So, what's this?"

"Your statement."

"I didn't know extortion was part of your job description."

"Isn't that a bit extravagant?"

"What? The word or the invoice?"

Abruptly, the lights flicked on. Danielle shuddered, her eyes adjusting to the sudden brightness. Slowly, she focused on seven men, one older.

"You're right, Rafi," the older one said with an explosive enthusiasm. "She is wonderful!"

Danielle looked directly at Rafi and then asked, "Who the hell are these people, Cardinel?"

"We're friends, Danielle," the older one said with a smile that Danielle's insights couldn't trust. No one is that happy. Her deduction: he wanted something.

"Oh, really? Whose?"

"I'm Herzog. We're friends who need your help."

"With what?" she asked.

"The diamond problem that's been plaguing our world, Danielle. Your father was killed by them."

Danielle's eyes narrowed as she slowly stepped toward him. "If you need help, I suggest you call the Mossad."

"Danielle," Rafi said, "we are the Mossad."

Danielle jerked her head to look at him, her eyes filled with contempt. *A setup. It was all a damn setup!* she thought. She glared back at Herzog.

Now she knew why the bogus bill from Cardinel—to set her up. She also knew why she was buzzed in without question. She was pissed, and that was the least of her feelings.

Finally, she asked, "And what if I say no?"

"That's your choice," Herzog said. "But I don't think you'd want everyone to know that Sam was not your biological father. You know how small the diamond community is."

Danielle threw a piercing look at Rafi.

Controlled shock was pressed upon his face like an iron on a patch. It was obvious he honestly didn't know any more than she did. That made him clear with her, but just for that, not for the manner in which he got her there.

She swiftly turned to do a faceoff with Herzog. "Blackmail? You people truly are ruthless."

Herzog smiled with fulfillment.

"Why me?" Danielle asked.

"Let's just say we believe in you."

"Yeah … right."

Danielle shook her head, not believing him, not to mention this entire situation.

She looked at each and every one of the people in the room one by one. They all seemed to be good men, even Rafi. Herzog, she thought, was an entirely different animal. Finally, she made her decision. "No," she said to Herzog. "I won't be intimidated with your Gestapo crap. Your sideshow doesn't interest me. You've got the wrong girl, and how in the hell did you know I wasn't Sam's biological daughter?"

"We know much about you, Danielle." Herzog's smile dropped as abruptly as it came. "That's your decision. We can't make you do anything you wouldn't want to do."

She smirked. "No, you can't. Besides, now that I know Sam wasn't my biological father, why the hell would I care? Small community or not, either way, Sam will come out smelling like a rose. But I must admit," she continued with interest, "it does put a clarity to my life thus far, so I must thank you for that."

Herzog stood his ground but was taken by her presence. He could see she was a strong woman, but curiosity made him wonder what made her that way. She could see it in his face and smiled.

"Interesting," he said. "Who stole your diamonds, Danielle?" Herzog asked.

"I haven't the faintest idea."

"I think not."

"Yes you do, Danielle," Rafi remarked. "And it just might be the answer we need."

Looking at Rafi, Danielle was almost at the end of her rope, hanging by frays. "Prove it or find out for yourself."

Danielle turned her eyes back to Herzog. They gazed at each other for a challenging moment. Then Herzog said, "Gentlemen, it's time to go. Danielle," he said during a quick turn, "you're staying with Rafi while you're in Israel. Your bag has already been delivered." He stopped for a moment to look at her and said, "Sam was killed by this group, and I won't take that chance with you."

"I thought this country was safe."

"Things change," Herzog said, smiling.

"What's that supposed to mean?"

Herzog shrugged his shoulders and said, "Find out for yourself."

Danielle could only give him an indignant glare.

Herzog turned and gathered the others as Danielle and Rafi watched them leave. Having enough game playing, when the room was empty, Danielle looked at Rafi, and said, "And extortion isn't extravagant."

Danielle turned and walked from the room.

After taking a deep breath, Rafi grabbed his coat and briefcase and headed for the elevators to be with Danielle.

When the elevator arrived, they stepped into the car, and Rafi pressed the bottom button. Danielle pulled a pack of cigarettes from her pocket and lit one immediately.

Rafi asked, "Is there any place you don't smoke?"

"Is there any place you don't lie?" Danielle asked as she lit the cigarette and blew out the toxic smoke that filled the car.

Rafi tried to wave the smoke away but to no avail; it was there to stay, which made Danielle very happy.

In the underground garage, Rafi opened the passenger door for Danielle, and she turned and gazed at him with disappointment. "I'll never trust you again, Cardinel."

"I never thought you ever did."

They gazed at each other for a long, repugnant moment. Danielle then got into the car, and Rafi shut the door.

He briskly walked to the other side, got in, and started the engine. He looked at Danielle for a moment while the car warmed up. She was looking out the windshield, and her gaze never wavered. Irritated, a silent snort left his nostrils as he put the car in gear and drove out of the garage.

Danielle felt betrayed. How could Rafi? How could he? And how long had he been a Mossad agent? How long had he led this double life? Did Sam know? She couldn't wait to get into bed, alone, and grind all these questions in peace and quiet. So many emotions were bombarding her all at once that she didn't know what to say, so she said nothing.

Next stop, Rafi's.

Chapter Nine

DeViamond's chateau was a mammoth structure of conceit built in the seventeenth century. There were three turrets—two along the east wall and the other in the front just off center. It was a long chateau as well as tall. A moat ran around the foot of the building. This was DeViamond family home. But old families were like old civilizations; they died. DeViamond was no exception. He was the last.

Sasal sat in front of the massive fireplace that had elegant molding along the edges. It lay in the middle of the right wall of the great hall. Eight large grates could have sufficiently held a roaring blaze, but there were only three. Nevertheless, he enjoyed his small fire while having his afternoon brandy. He heard DeViamond's footsteps echo throughout the room of Louis IV furnishings with seven separate conversational areas. Frankly, it looked more like a hotel lobby for a French whore's convention.

"Sasal, there you are."

DeViamond walked over to him and took a seat in the chair next to his. He held letters and a magazine in his hand.

"The mail came, and there's a letter I thought you'd want to read." He took out a long envelope from the group and handed it to Sasal.

Sasal looked at the return address. It read: L.S., PO Box 271, London, SW13 9LW, England. He opened it and read the letter. It was what he'd been waiting for.

"A shipment is due in one veek." Sasal looked at DeViamond. "Are ve ready?"

"We've just been waiting for you."

He handed him the letter. "Do it."

DeViamond smiled. "I'll make the arrangements."

✳ ✳ ✳

Danielle listened to Rafi lock his front door as they stood on the top landing of the foyer stairs. The house was in old Jaffa and had an ornate Arabian Night sort of feel to it. The foyer had a twenty-foot ceiling, and the staircase had twenty steps with a wrought-iron banister. The entire foyer seemed to be a room unto itself with a Moroccan-style chandelier hanging from the middle.

Danielle walked down the stairs and through an arched doorway to the large living/dining area. It too had a Moroccan feel. A tapestry couch with leather chairs to either side and a coffee table sat in front of a fireplace. A long, engraved table, with matching embossed chairs, sat to the back in the dining area.

Rafi followed her into the room and tossed his coat to the back of the couch as Danielle looked the place over, remembering from the last time she was there. Not much had changed except for a Moroccan-style screen he'd added. It had to be authentic; Rafi always bought the real deal. It was nice. She remembered him having three bedrooms, though one of them might as well be considered a very large closet. Rafi used it as a store room for other antiques. *Not bad,* she thought as she walked to the center of the room. He did have class; she'd give him that. But now things had changed between them, at least as far as she was concerned. He had deceived her. Besides that, he was Mossad, and she could tell he took it seriously rather than seeing it as an adventure. He was definitely committed.

She flatly looked at him. "Gemologist, entrepreneur, spy … My but we are a multifaceted individual, aren't we?"

Rafi silently gave her an eye and then walked across the room to a painting of a rabbi at the Wailing Wall. He pulled it open like a door on hinges and revealed a safe. *That is new,* Danielle thought. *Trite but new.*

Rafi opened the safe, took out a long, black box, turned, and faced her. "I thought you said your stones were stolen."

"They were. You were there. They're gone, Cardinel."

He held out the box to her. "Then what's this?"

A good five seconds passed before she stepped to him to retrieve the box. She looked at it and then at him.

"Open it," he said, as if encouraging her.

Taking a breath, she let it out slowly as she lifted the lid, her eyes never wavering from his.

"Look at it," he insisted as he took a seat on the edge of his desk.

She lifted the lid and then looked inside. Suddenly, her eyes widened in disbelief, and she said, "Give me a jeweler's loop."

He already had one handy and held it out to her with one finger.

In one stride, she was at his side, the loop in her hand. She put the box on the desk and picked up one of the stones. With the loop to her eye, she began to sight the stone. A myriad of emotions swept over her like a rush of adrenaline. "That bastard," she snarled.

"They weren't stolen! You sent them!"

"Why in the hell would I send you my stones, and this better be good?" Her voice dared him.

"You knew what Sam was planning. You said it yourself that there'd be surprises."

"Look, doll, I can think of a few more poignant tasks of retribution I could have taken—especially against you—and this isn't one of them!"

Danielle could see Rafi thinking. He was brushing the underside of his mustache, his face sober, staring her down. He was frustrated; that she could see.

"Then Sam must have sent them himself," Rafi noted.

"When did you retrieve this little grab bag?"

"A week ago."

"Funny, Sam's been dead for two months."

Rafi thought again. She could see his eyes wandering as if looking for an answer. "Then he had someone else send them for him."

"In other words, Sam knew he was going to be murdered, set it up with whoever, and they sent the stones … right. But I'll tell you what," Danielle said as she dropped the loop and stone back into Rafi's hand, "you call me when you've got it all figured out, Mr. Bond. I'm going to bed. Don't worry, I can find my way."

Danielle was done with this bullshit, which is exactly what she thought—bullshit.

Rafi's eyes narrowed as he watched her walk through the open arch to a small bedroom hallway at the back and disappeared.

He looked at the stones in the velvet box with more questions than answers, and he didn't like it—not one little bit.

* * *

The next morning, Rafi sat behind his desk at work, the winter rain keeping him from focusing on his work. The rain pounded against the windows, like how he felt. He looked out the window at the sea. *No swimmers today,* he thought and leaned back in his chair. The diamonds from Goren's he had received in the mail lay heavy on his mind. It was a mystery how they were stolen and now how they came to him. Danielle honestly didn't know how they came to him as well. He could tell that; she would have nothing to gain if she had. She told the truth. So how did those damn things end up with him?

Dear God, he screamed in his head. "What the hell is going on?"

He pounded his fist on his desk top in frustration, but it was a futile attempt to understand what was in front of him. And Danielle was no help.

Danielle, he thought. She made him think of her father Sam, and how they met. It was at Rafi's mother's funeral about eighteen years before. Sam was the one who found him and told his story of Rafi's mother and him. Sam had told Rafi his mother and he were very close, and he mourned her as if she'd been his daughter. Sam continued to tell Rafi how he'd known her in the late fifties when Israel was young. The story of Rafi's mother was about her diamonds that she'd smuggled out from Amsterdam during the Nazi regime in the hem of her dress, which totaled two hundred carats.

Her name was Sarah, and Sam was the one who helped her start up her diamond business with one cutter and herself years later. It was during the story that Sam pulled out a photo of her he'd always carried. Rafi remembered being so touched by Sam and his photo that he took to Sam like a best friend once lost. Sam talked incessantly of Rafi's mother. Rafi could feel how much this man loved her.

He told Rafi that he unfortunately couldn't stay and left for America. Sam gave an excuse that was fairly lame, but Sarah believed in him and let it pass. Rafi and his mother were close. She taught him the business, and that's what he did. The business was growing little by little. Rafi had never known his father, and his mother never spoke of him. Rafi was fine with that, though curiosity made him wonder occasionally. His mother told him that his father had died, and Rafi accepted that. He was still curious about his father, she never talked about him once.

It was at the funeral that Sam took Rafi under his supervision, and Rafi was more than willing to take it. From then on, they were close, especially because of the relationship between Sam and his mother. Rafi kept a picture of his mother at home, not at his office. His office was for business; his home was for memories.

Rafi turned to look back out the window at the gray day. He wondered what Israel was like back then and how different it must have been compared to today. He sighed. It was different all right, and Danielle wasn't helping.

Chapter Ten

Mathew Somner was assigned to the shipping and scheduling department at DeVorhes—the most sacred of all departments. The British felt there must be a leak from within; too many couriers were being knocked off too effectively. Hardly anything was finding their routes. It was beginning to hurt the company as well as the rest of the buyers and not only monetarily.

He kept a close eye on all the employees but mostly the secretaries. Someone had to be consorting with the enemy. He had to find out who. He hoped it wouldn't take long. Time was short, he remembered Herzog saying, and it was. He'd go back to work that night. DeVorhes knew he was a plant, so Somner was open twenty-four hours a day. Whatever it took, he'd find it, including bugging the phones and the secretary's pool, not to mention the mail room.

Someone knew too much, and he or she was talking—talking to the wrong people.

* * *

Goren's was busy that morning. All the sales rooms were full. The head salesman, Stan Engman, was no exception. A slender man in his early forties with dark hair, Stan was a likable guy who knew the business well. He'd been with the company since he was in his twenties but had learned more from Danielle than anyone else. He was with one of Goren's best customers, Isaac Goldman, a peach of a fellow who had the full measurements to match.

They were in a sales room that was twelve-by-twelve with a desk, two chairs on either side, and on the table a lamp that gave off white light and a pencil holder with pencils and small sheets of paper. Stan gave Goldman his three paper pouches. Goldman opened one and took out a jeweler's loop and sighted a stone. He smiled. He did the same to the other two pouches, and his smile grew. Stan was pleased. He knew Goldman was ready and primed.

Stan took a sheet of paper and wrote down a figure, folded the paper, and waited for Goldman to do the same. They then exchanged their bids. Stan thought he'd start high, since Goldman seemed so happy with the goods. They looked at each other's bids. Goldman looked at Stan and waved a finger. Stan laughed. They did the same thing again. This time Stan lowered his bid, and Goldman upped his. Stan looked at Goldman's bid as Goldman looked at Stan's bid. Goldman thought for a few moments as he gazed at the bid from Stan. The big man then smiled and put out his hand. They shook. The deal was done.

✳ ✳ ✳

Boris hurried through the front door of Goren's and down the hall past the sales rooms and the file cabinets by his desk. He was late. The New York traffic of hurry up and wait was too routine but somehow worse today. Then he saw Marvin standing by his desk as he passed the cabinets.

"You're late," Marvin said.

"Tell me," Boris remarked as he rounded his desk, took off his coat, and hung it up on the coat rack.

"How long do you think Danny will be gone?" Marvin asked.

"She didn't say when she called a few days ago."

"She didn't leave any messages for me?"

"Not one word, but she sounded a little out of sorts. Why are you asking now?"

"Just curious."

Boris sat down at his desk and pulled the top middle drawer again. Unfortunately, it only opened halfway.

"Damn this desk! I've been playing good day, bad day with this desk for five years. Sometimes it opens and sometimes it doesn't."

"You want me to try it?"

"Go ahead. It hasn't listened to me today. Obviously this is a bad day. Good luck."

Marvin took hold of the handle and jerked the drawer so hard that it not only opened but threw everything on the floor.

Boris looked at Marvin, and Marvin said, "Well, at least it's open."

Boris just sighed and bent over to pick up pens, pencils, and anything a secretary would need. Out of guilt, Marvin helped. But as he looked up at Boris to give him the materials, he noticed something hanging from underneath the desk's top from inside the drawer.

"Boris, what's that?" he asked as he pointed to what looked like a book hanging by masking tape from underneath.

"What's what?"

"There, inside where the drawer would be."

Boris looked and then stuck his hand in and pulled out a black book with tape around it. He brought it out.

"What the hell?" said Boris as he opened the book, which only had numbers throughout each page. "Look at this, Marvin."

Marvin took the book and looked as he thumbed through the pages. Each page had nothing but numbers and didn't make sense.

"Where did Danny say she was staying?" Marvin asked.

"She didn't say."

"She needs to know about this."

"I'll call Rafi. He might be in his office still. He'd know where she'd be."

* * *

At Rafi's home, Danielle stood in the doorway of the bedroom hallway, peering at a man sitting on the couch, his back to her. He had dark hair, slightly wavy, and for some reason seemed young, at least to her. Her eyes narrowed. A babysitter, she thought.

The rain was still falling. She could hear it on the line of windows that looked out onto the patio. She'd just woken up. Jet lag had finally set in. Darkness had fallen, for the only light that was on was a lamp on the side table next to the couch. At least she was dressed, wearing jeans and a black turtleneck sweater. And shoes were a must. The floor was cold tiles of terrazzo, though Persian rugs were scattered throughout.

She pushed her hair away from her face and wondered who was there. Obviously he heard her and turned around to see. As she came closer, she remembered him from Rafi's office that first night she was there.

"Good morning, Danielle. Or maybe I should say good evening," he said with a hand extended.

"Say what you like. Just don't say you're my babysitter and we'll be friends."

As he dropped his hand, Danielle noticed he was wearing a gun in a shoulder holster inside his jacket. Suddenly, she felt like a hostage.

"I'm Erez," he told her.

"I'm happy for you. Now where's Cardinel?"

"At his office."

"Which one?"

His smile dropped, and he said, "His."

The phone rang, and Erez answered. "Cardinel's residence."

He listened for a moment and then handed the receiver to Danielle while he held the phone. "It's for you."

Danielle put the receiver to her ear and said, "Yes?"

"Danny," she heard on the other end.

"Boris? What are you doing calling me here?"

"Rafi told me you'd be at this number. I had to tell you!" He sounded out of sorts. "I found out what was jamming my drawer."

He continued to tell her about the book. Danielle's brow furrowed, and she said, "Drop what you're doing and get to El Al and have it on that plane. Address it to Rafi. Send it now!" she told him and hung up.

She knew he'd do as he was told immediately if she hung up.

She turned back to Erez and handed him the receiver.

"What was that all about?" Erez asked as he put the phone back on the table, seeming more than just interested.

Danielle just sighed as she took a seat on the back of the couch. "A broken heart and my draft card."

* * *

A day later, Rafi stretched and then turned off his desk lamp. The day was done. It was a little after six p.m., and he began to put papers in order for him to look at the next morning. Then he heard a knock at his door. Just as he looked up, his secretary walked in with a package.

"This just came for you on the late delivery."

Rafi took the box and said, "Thank you."

"Is there anything else?" she asked.

"No. But thank you for staying late."

"No problem. See you in the morning."

"Good night."

"Good night."

Hadasah walked out of his office but left the door open. She knew Rafi could hear everything that would or wouldn't happen in the office.

He took his letter opener, cut through the tape, and opened the box. Pushing back the panels of the box, he saw parcels of paper pouches. He didn't need to open a one of them; he knew what they were. But he did open one pouch and found uncut diamonds and the size that his company handled. Someone knew him and his company well. He didn't like that. He found a note inside.

With a pair of jeweler's tweezers, he picked up the note and laid it on the desktop. From a drawer, he picked out a small plastic bag and placed the note inside. Strange notes weren't the only oddities that passed by his desk, but since this diamond affair, it seemed notes and diamonds were the norm. It was just like the other three boxes he'd received. He'd take the note to Herzog. They probably wouldn't find anything, but what else could he do?

Rafi taped the box back up and walked down the hall to the cutters' room where the vault stood. They'd be safe for the night, and in the morning he'd send them over to Carl Jacobson in Haifa for analysis. Every diamond had its own markings, like the rings on a tree. Carl would know not necessarily who sent them but at least the region they came from. Someone was taking care of him during this crisis, and he wanted to know who. He hoped the results wouldn't come back like last time. He'd stop off at Herzog's at headquarters on his way home. He knew he'd be there. His couch wasn't just for sitting on.

✷ ✷ ✷

Herzog was sitting at his desk on the phone when Rafi stepped just inside his office. Herzog looked up and motioned for him to enter. Rafi walked to the desk just as Herzog hung up.

"Rafi, that was Somner. He thinks he has three possibilities."

"Good. Has he been compromised?"

"He doesn't think so," Herzog answered and then looked at him a bit more personably. "What is it? You look as if you'd just been slapped in the face, which reminds me." He smirked. "How's our guest?"

"Trying," he said. "How long do you expect me to keep her here?"

"Long enough for something to rear its ugly head."

"Well, I think you just got your wish."

Rafi held up the plastic bag with the note inside. Herzog's smile dropped.

He took the bag and read the note aloud. "In your time of need." He looked back at Rafi. "Another mystery package?"

Rafi nodded. "It came in the late delivery. I'm having Carl check them out tomorrow. There's enough for three months easy."

"Someone likes you."

"Or is playing with me."

Herzog looked at the bag again. "I'll take this to the lab, though I doubt we'll find anything, but it's worth a try."

"So, what do I do with Danielle?" Rafi asked.

Herzog smiled, seeming to be enjoying Rafi's predicament. "Have her teach you about Goren's. She has to anyway."

"You still want her here?"

"Absolutely. Don't worry," Herzog chuckled as he patted Rafi on the back. "She'll come in handy, I know it."

"Yes, sir," was all Rafi could say.

"Go home and relieve Erez. I'm sure he's had his fill today."

Rafi just nodded and left the office.

Chapter Eleven

Sasal sat at a lovely Louis IVX desk in DeViamond's library. The library itself was large, with two walls full of books. A balcony or mezzanine ran across on the side with a spiral staircase from the corner. Velvet curtains hung the entire length of the balcony, hiding the entire wall, the spiral staircase seeming to go nowhere. He was scratching in his account books, writing notes in the margins, and calculating this and that from date to date. Things needed to be stepped up, he felt. The couriers were growing tiresome, and they needed to get their point across more quickly—more definitely. The next few days couldn't come soon enough.

DeViamond walked in and took a seat in one of the chairs in front of the desk holding an open letter. "How do things look?" DeViamond asked, his monocle to his eye.

"Goot, but ve need to do better."

"Amsterdam was a success. So were three other major cities."

"Dhat's not goot enough anymore. Ve need to hit dhem and hit dhem hard."

"That shipment is coming up. That'll hit them hard." DeViamond smiled.

"I vant him informed again. Just to make sure. Now, bring me Lydia's book. Dhe little black one."

"Whatever for?"

Being a stickler for details, Sasal said, "I vant to keep dhe books together. Besides, I vant to analyze dhe schedules."

DeViamond sighed with a shrug. "All right, but I don't think it's necessary." Then the thought came to him of why he wanted to talk. "Another letter came today." He held up the typed page.

"Did you read it?"

"Yes. Lydia thinks there may be a spy inside DeVorhes."

Sasal looked up at him. "A spy? Does she know who he is?"

"She's not sure, but a couple of new people have been assigned to her office. She's checking them out."

Sasal nodded. "She'll keep us informed."

"I'll get that book, and make that call."

✳ ✳ ✳

It was around sunset when Gram Morse sat at a folding table in the hanger amongst DeVorhes's private fleet of two Gulfstream Fives and three Global Expresses with five other men. He was the kind of guy you'd trust just from his wide grin and cozy demeanor. He looked like a little prize fighter with his bomber jacket on, though he was a pilot for DeVorhes. But his smile was absent at that moment as he was sitting in the middle of a poker game with three mechanics and two other pilots. He had a flush and had no intention of giving that away.

"I'll see ya and raise you five," one of the mechanics said as he threw in his chips to the middle of the table and then looked at Morse.

Morse rubbed his chin as if thinking and said, "I'll see ya and raise ya ten." He threw his chips in on the middle pile.

A jingle of "God Save the Queen" rang on Morse's cell phone, and he answered it. "Hello," he said. His eyes brightened as he listened for a moment and then put his hand over the bottom half of the cell. Glancing at the men, he said, "It's my mum." He went back to the conversation, knowing the men were listening. "Good to hear from ya, Mum. I'll see ya in a short while, ya know." He winked at the men. "I'd love that, and you will too. Listen, dear, I'm in the middle of something, so I need to go." He listened again as his smile grew, showing his pearly whites. "Love to you too, Mum. Bye." He looked at the group as he snapped his phone shut and put it away.

He rubbed his hands together and then showed his cards. Everyone groaned, threw down their cards, and watched Morse pull all the chip towards him. Now, he could smile that trusting smile he was known for.

* * *

DeViamond slyly snickered as he hung up the phone.

* * *

It was around seven at night when Danielle and Erez heard the front door open. Danielle was sitting in one of the chairs in Rafi's living room area reading the *Jerusalem Post*. She hadn't been out of the townhouse for three days but still found refuge on Rafi's patio to have a smoke. The patio was safe because it was the end of a cliff which reached the sea.

Erez pulled his gun, but Danielle said, "It's Rafi, Mr. Mossad. Relax."

At least she liked Erez. He seemed to be a nice guy and had her safety in mind. He pulled out his gun like he'd done it many times before. She was glad he was on her side. He reminded her of a little boy with a big toy. He was a little too serious for her, but a nice guy.

Rafi popped inside the arched doorway. He stopped and looked at Erez with his gun drawn.

"I told you," Danielle said as she continued to read.

Erez put it back into his holster, and said, "Sorry, Raf."

Rafi had his briefcase and two white bags with him. Danielle looked at the bags as a slight groan grazed the back of her throat. Rafi placed his briefcase on the dining table with the bags.

"Let me guess," Danielle began as she put her paper on the couch. "Falafels again."

"Chinese." Rafi held up the bags.

Danielle's face soured. "Hell, Cardinel, you can't cook, you drive a shitty car, and you lie! You're going to make a great catch."

"Flattery will get you nowhere."

"Who's flattering? It's the damn truth."

Erez chuckled, and then as Rafi looked at him, he stopped, covering his mouth, and said, "Sorry, Raf."

Erez found the two of them as if fighters in a ring, both well matched to the other. He wondered if it always was like this with them.

Rafi rolled his eyes at Danielle's comment and opened the bags. "Just be happy I'm feeding you," he noted.

"Just be happy I'm here to feed."

He looked at her with a look of seriousness. He knew she was right. She could say, "Screw you" and jump back to New York. Then Danielle grinned. Rafi was trying to play the tough guy. She figured she must be aggravating him too much, which was fine with her. As far as she was concerned, he deserved to be aggravated—especially by her.

"One is Mongolian beef with fried rice, and the other is chicken lo mein. Your choice."

Before Danielle could come to a conclusion, a knock on the door caught everyone's attention. Erez immediately pulled his gun again, but Rafi held out his hand for him to put it back.

"Trigger happy, Erez?" Danielle asked with a smirk as she headed for the table and brought out one of the Chinese containers that read "thank you" in Hebrew. She got a kick out of that.

Rafi left to answer the door.

"By the way, Danielle, I'm here to protect you," said Erez.

"From what?"

Then Danielle saw that the footsteps heard were from Rafi and Herzog. She groaned again from within. Danielle looked at Erez and said, "I see your point."

"It's Herzog," Erez commented.

"Exactly."

Herzog had one of those smiles that only a Lugar could love. He held a small package in his hands and walked to Danielle and held it out. "I believe this is for you. It just came off the last flight from El Al."

Danielle took it and looked at the return address. It was from Boris. "Nicely confiscated," she remarked.

"Let's say personally delivered," Herzog said.

"It's actually for you." Danielle handed it back to him. She then crossed her arms, as if wanting nothing to do with it. "Open it. I'm sure you'll find it enlightening."

Rafi slipped off his leather blazer, threw it on the back of a dining chair, and then stepped to Herzog and Danielle.

Herzog opened the small package and found a little black leather-bound book with thin pages. His features sobered. He slipped off his gloves and tossed them onto the table. Instantly, he began thumbing through the pages of numbers. He looked at Danielle and asked, "What is this?"

"I was hoping you could tell me."

Rafi asked, "Where did you get this?"

"Boris found it, and I had him send it. It was the reason why his desk drawer stuck some of the time." She looked at Herzog. "It was found in Lydia's desk that Boris took over."

"Who's Lydia?" Herzog asked.

"Sam's old secretary," she answered and then looked at Rafi.

Danielle could see Herzog thinking pensively for a moment, and then he said, "Erez, call Moshe. I want him to take a look at this."

"Why?" Rafi asked, becoming belligerent. "It could mean anything, not just a code."

"Like what, Cardinel?" Danielle remarked more than questioned.

"It could be shipping dates," Rafi retorted.

"Then where's the name of the wholesaler, doll?"

Rafi stood silent, his jaw clenched. Danielle could see he wasn't going to take this laying down. She knew how much he believed in Sam and how much he hoped it wasn't what it seemed.

"I'll get on it, sir," Erez said and went to the phone and dialed.

"Well, one way or another we'll know," Herzog said as he continued to flip through the book, shaking his head. He then looked at Danielle. "Welcome to the team, my dear."

"I'm not part of the team. I'm just a lowly informer."

"Of course, Danielle." Herzog smiled.

Chapter Twelve

In DeViamond's library, the moonlight shone through the tall, thin windows as if flying buttresses were holding up the wall. Sasal was going over shipping schedules at the desk. Everything seemed to be irregular, as if DeVorhes was trying to thwart the killers on the streets. They hadn't succeeded. Lydia had done a good job of keeping them informed on changes from day one. She was better than a St. Bernard sniffing out more than brandy.

Suddenly, DeViamond crashed through the doors, anxious and out of breath.

"Sasal, I can't find that book anywhere. It's not in any of her boxes, and it's not in the lower-level office either."

"Vhat?" Sasal exclaimed as he snapped the tip of his pencil on the paper. "It has to be!"

"I'm sorry, but it isn't. I spent the entire day looking for it. Sasal, it's not here!"

Sasal thought for a moment. There was only one place it could be. "It's at Goren's. Danielle has it. It's been five years, and I need dhat book now!"

"I doubt that. She wouldn't know what it was even if she did have it. You give her too much credit."

"And you don't give her enough!" He thought another moment, then looked at DeViamond, and said, "Send Hans and Olan." Sasal smiled, thinking of the two. When he found that the two could shoot and didn't care what at, he found more engaging things for them to do. "Have dhem take care of it. She alvays vorks late."

"You just can't kill her, Sasal."

"Sam vas murdered, vhy not her?"

DeViamond tipped his head as he put his monocle to his eye. Sasal knew DeViamond would go along with him. He always did.

Just then, a butler came into the room with a small, silver tray with an envelope. He walked to DeViamond and held it out as he slightly bowed. "This just came for you, sir."

DeViamond took the envelope, and the butler walked from the room. It was a telegram. He opened it.

"Look at this," DeViamond said to Sasal as he handed it off.

Sasal took a look at it. It was an address and nothing more. "Lydia found our spy," Sasal said as he dropped it on the desk. "Have our London team pick him up tonight. Our fireworks begin tomorrow. Ve don't need him getting in our vay."

DeViamond nodded. "Done."

* * *

It was around eight in the evening when Mathew Somner walked down his street of neat row houses with English gardens in front of each house. Somner was slight in build and in his thirties. He'd been with the secret service for three years. This was his most unusual assignment. There were so many people to choose from, but he'd narrowed it down to two. Soon he expected to find the one giving DeVorhes's secrets away.

As he walked to the front of his fenced yard, a van pulled up. He turned to look. Abruptly, the side door slid open as four men bolted out and surrounded him. He tried to fight them off, but he was hooded and dragged into the van. Once inside, he felt a needle pierce his skin, and then he fell limp. The van sped away as the side door closed.

* * *

At Cardinel Limited, Rafi sat behind his desk looking over the faxes of the last four quarters of Goren's books. Erez sat on the couch reading a magazine from the industry, while Danielle leaned a shoulder against the windows and looked out at the blue sky. Amazingly, the rain had broken, though the temperature was still only in the fifties. God only knew how Danielle hated winter no matter where she was.

"Marvin only sent me last year's quotas."

"Criminy, Cardinel, how far back do you need to go?"

Rafi just shook his head, gave her a look, and then went back to the pages. "It says here that there was a margin jump in January." He turned and looked at Danielle.

"After Christmas sale," she remarked, still looking at the sea.

His face slightly tensed. "You sound like a retailer."

"It moves product."

Rafi silently snorted through his nostrils and went back to his pages. Then the phone rang, and Rafi picked up.

"Cardinel."

"Rafi," he heard on the other end, "Herzog. Get down here at once." He sounded more than agitated. That wasn't like him.

"Right away." Rafi hung up as he stood and turned to look at Danielle. "We'll have to go over this later. Erez will take you home. I'll be back with you as soon as possible. Until then, Erez will take care of you."

Danielle lifted a brow. "Careful, Cardinel. You're beginning to sound like we care about each other."

Rafi said nothing as Erez and Danielle walked from the room.

* * *

At Mossad Headquarters, Herzog was on the phone again when Rafi stepped into his office. Herzog motioned for him to come in and close the door. As he did, Herzog hung up and turned his attentions to Rafi.

"I just talked to Nibbons. Somner didn't check in last night and wasn't at work today. They think he's been kidnapped." Herzog shook his head as he began to pace back and forth. "It looks like their mole found our mole first."

"Will he talk?"

"I was told he wouldn't."

"What do you think?"

"We're screwed. He hasn't been in the service that long. Who knows what tactics they've taught him," Herzog stated, rubbing his forehead as seriousness seemed to rip at his features.

Rafi knew Herzog had as much faith in the British as he did the CIA—not much.

"I have a feeling we're beginning to play cat and mouse, and we're the mouse," Herzog retorted.

"How long ago did you find this out?"

"Right before I called you."

Rafi looked at his watch. It was around two in the afternoon. The call from Herzog came thirty minutes before. "So now what?"

Herzog looked at Rafi with sternness in his features. "We wait. There's nothing more we can do at this point. By the way, Moshe is coming to your place tonight. I've got him working on a few other things, so it'll be around nine."

"You still think that book is coded?" Rafi wasn't convinced.

"We'll soon see. By the way, I'm contacting the others. They should be on high alert. There's no telling what may happen next. I'm also having Goren's tapped. If anything should happen, we'll know."

"Do you really think that's necessary?"

"I sincerely do. If these people can kill from almost anywhere in the world, knock off couriers at their whim, they're bigger than we ever expected."

Rafi wrinkled his brow. He never thought of it in those terms. "Have any more couriers been taken?"

"No, and that's what worries me. I think they're going for higher stakes, but I don't know what. We don't have enough intel to determine how big they are. Small teams hitting top men and couriers is one thing. But what else, I don't know."

"Well, we know they're big enough to go to London from their base and snatch Somner."

Herzog sighed. "Rafi, we don't even know where their base is." He started to pace again and then stopped and looked at Rafi. "Go home, and take care of Danielle. She just might be next if that book contains anything juicy."

"Call me if anything comes up. I'll be home."

Herzog nodded. "Just keep an eye on Danielle. Saying she might be next doesn't feel like just a threat anymore. It's a reality."

Rafi thought about that comment. Suddenly, he felt responsible for Danielle's welfare—something he'd never felt for her before. How foreign.

* * *

As Rafi drove home, he thought about how he had always believed Danielle could take care of herself, no matter what. He almost thought of her as a sophisticated pit bull. But they were dealing with a whole different animal. Now it seemed it was up to him. It was something neither of them could taste, hear, or see ... at least thus far. But Danielle needing *his* protection? He honestly didn't know how to react. It could have been a laugh if it weren't so damn serious. Yet, in a strange sort of way, it felt good.

Traffic wasn't too bad. He'd be home in less than twenty minutes, but first he had to make a stop. For once he'd make dinner for her. Nothing extravagant; just enough to make her take note. She didn't know everything about him, though she'd like to think she did. He felt good knowing Erez was with her. He was a crack shot and had a good head. With Somner gone, it seemed these people could be anywhere—even the Middle East.

He realized he had to play this cool. He didn't want her to feel as if the ceiling could cave in at any moment. He pulled open his glove compartment and reached for his gun. At a stop light, which in Israel is only a suggestion, he slid the holster onto his belt with his weapon and then pulled his turtleneck's bottom ribbing over his gun. He looked at his watch. Herzog was making him edgy with all this talk. And that's what he hoped it was—talk. Now for that stop.

* * *

Rafi locked the door and came down the foyer stairs with his briefcase in one hand and a woven plastic mesh bag in the other, all with assorted items. He walked into the living area and was met by Erez and his gun staring him down. A look of surprise came to Erez's face. It wasn't Rafi's usual time to come home.

"You're home early. What's the occasion?" Danielle asked as she shut the patio door and walked to the desk in front of the French doors.

"I took the rest of the day off," Rafi said as he placed his briefcase on the dining table, along with his plastic carry. He looked at Erez. "I can take it from here."

"You're sure?" he asked as he put his weapon back.

Rafi held up his hand and said, "I'm sure. Go home."

Erez nodded. "Then tomorrow," he said. "Have a nice evening, you two."

Danielle smiled at him. "Tomorrow I'll let you beat me at chess."

Erez just smiled and headed for the foyer. Rafi followed as Danielle went for the plastic carry to see what was in it. She found peppers, wrapped meat of some kind, couscous, and a bottle of red wine. Hearing footsteps come to an end, she turned to see Rafi standing in the arched doorway.

Danielle took her hand out of the carry and asked, "So, why are you home so early?"

"Can't I take an afternoon off?"

"It's your company."

Rafi showed a hint of a smile. "I thought we'd have an early dinner."

"An early dinner? Does that mean you're cooking?"

"It does."

Danielle lightly slapped herself on her cheek as if taken aback. "Oh, heart be still. The man can cook?"

Rafi chuckled openly.

Danielle widened her smile when she heard the unfamiliar sound come from his mouth. "My God! He laughs too!"

"See," he said as he pointed his finger. "You don't know everything about me." His chuckle turned into a large smile.

"I still know you drive a shitty car and lie."

"Would you have come to Israel if I asked you to?"

"No, but you still could have asked."

Rafi just nodded with a knowing smile and then said, "Let me change. We're grilling tonight."

"And what, pray tell, are we grilling?"

"Lamb."

* * *

Rafi sat at the head of the table with Danielle to his side on the right eating lamb kabobs and couscous. The meat was succulent, the peppers sweet and crisp, and the couscous delicate and flakey. Danielle was impressed. Rafi had cooked for her and was being a gentleman. No arguing, no sarcasm; they were civil to one another. He'd almost done a 180, and Danielle just followed his lead. But she wondered what brought about his sudden change in disposition.

"More wine?" Rafi asked.

"Please." She held up her glass.

As Rafi reached for the wine bottle, she saw the butt of his gun as his sweater lifted. A sudden surge of apprehension rushed through her body. She'd never seen him wear a gun before. She didn't even know a gun was in the house. In Israel, civilians couldn't own a gun, but then, he wasn't a civilian. She couldn't help but wonder what was up and what the phone call was about that made him kick her out of his office so fast in the afternoon. Did that have anything to do with the sudden urge to wear a firearm? It felt scary, yet awesome. *How curious,* she thought.

"How's dinner?" Rafi asked as he poured the wine.

"I wouldn't kick you out of my bed, if that's what you're asking."

He smiled. "Thank you. There's more if you like."

"No, really, I'm completely full. But tell me, Mr. CEO, who's running Goren's in my absence?" she asked, knowing she'd ask about the gun later.

Rafi looked at her from under his eyebrows as his elbows found the tabletop and answered, "Three people: Stan, Boris, and Marvin."

Danielle raised an eyebrow in relief. "Good choice." She sat back in her chair and crossed her arms. Now her next question. "Why is Erez here every day?"

"For your protection."

She took a breath through her nostrils and let it out the same way. That wasn't quite what she expected to hear. She felt there was some truth in the matter, but she also knew the brass ring hadn't been caught yet. "Why can't I go home?" she finally asked.

"For your protection."

Danielle dropped her shoulders with a harsh sigh. "You mean Herzog wants me here for some nefarious reason."

Rafi eluded the remark by saying, "By the way, you can smoke in the house. I don't want you on the patio anymore."

"Let me guess. My protection."

Rafi chewed his last bite, swallowed, and said, "Quite frankly, yes."

"Is that why you're wearing a gun?"

Rafi looked at her as if he'd been caught with his hand in the cookie jar but refused to answer.

Danielle picked up her fork, played in her couscous for a moment, looked at him, and finally decided to ask, "What was up with that call you got this afternoon?" There was no other explanation for Rafi's gun-toting and gracious behavior.

Rafi looked at her for a good while. She knew then and there he wasn't going to tell her, at least not the truth. But he finally answered.

"It doesn't concern you, Danielle. Just like my gun," he said. Then he picked up both plates and walked into the kitchen.

She couldn't believe that and downed her wine. What more could she do?

* * *

Shafts of light filtered through the great hall's windows, staining the marble floor with translucent white. It was late in the day. Sasal sat in front of the fireplace, enjoying a brandy while he waited for the word. He looked up at DeViamond, who stood with his arm above the mantel as if ready for his portrait to be taken.

"Vell?" Sasal asked DeViamond.

DeViamond casually brought out his pocket watch and looked at it. "Now," he answered as he peered at Sasal with his monocle to his eye and a smirk upon his thin lips.

Sasal sipped his brandy and relaxed into his chair.

Soon the wait would be over. Success was all he needed.

Chapter Thirteen

T he co-pilot had thrown the master switch, and the jet engines were now running. Standing just inside the door of the Gulfstream stood Gram Morse. With that appealing smile, he watched five hundred million dollars worth of diamonds board the plane carried by ten men, six with titanium briefcases handcuffed to their wrists, the other four armed guards. They all walked down the aisle and took all but two of the seats in the large cabin. Morse followed, instructing each of them to buckle up for the three-hour-and-twenty-minute trek. They'd be leaving Johannesburg within a few minutes. They would arrive at a small airport outside of Casablanca to refuel and then continue to London. It would be a large enough airfield to handle such a craft yet small enough not to care. Morse walked back down the aisle to close and lock the plane's door.

As he stepped into the cockpit, Morse took his seat as pilot and buckled himself in. After they were given the go ahead, he and his co-pilot, James McLain, a DeVorhes trusted veteran, pushed the power levers forward. At 140 miles per hour, the plane ascended into the sky and on its way toward North Africa, arriving around sunset.

The low ceiling of marshmallow cloud cover meant turbulence, for their ascent into the sky would bring them to forty thousand feet, though the craft could go up to fifty-eight thousand. Either way, until they rose above the clouds, it'd be a rough time but not too bad.

After a half an hour into the flight, Morse put the plane on auto pilot and then said to McLain, "How 'bout some coffee?"

"Sounds good. I'll get it."

"No. I'll get it. It's my turn anyway."

With cheek-to-cheek smile on Morse's face, McLain nodded. No one could resist that smile, and Morse knew it and used it to his advantage.

Morse unbuckled his seatbelt and walked from the cockpit into the cabin. He asked, "Anyone for coffee?"

Hands were raised as well, and a few "sure" and "me" were heard. He walked to the back of the cabin into the galley that was behind a door.

An institutional-style coffee maker sat on a counter. He placed the metal pot underneath and then retrieved a vial of white powder from the inside breast pocket of his bomber jacket. After taking out the cork from the vial, he poured the white powder into the metal pot. A smile came to his face as he opened the lid, poured in the water, put coffee in the bin, and turned it on. A Boy Scout grin crossed his lips as he listened to the start of the end. These boys wouldn't be just sleeping; they'd be sleeping the big sleep, with no rude awakenings. In fact, with no awakenings at all.

Things were progressing as they should. Adrenaline surged through his body, and it felt so good. It was almost like Christmas morning when he was a little boy. But then, the rewards were good as well. He watched the coffee blend with the cyanide, that Boy Scout grin curled on his lips again. *This is too easy,* he thought.

Morse poured the cups and took the tray to each man in the cabin. Then he put down the tray on a stand to the side of the cockpit's door. He picked up the last two cups and knocked on the door with his foot. Since the plane was on auto pilot, McLain opened the door for him.

"Hey, great," McLain said with a smile and took one of the cups.

"The pilot has to take care of his cargo, doesn't he?" Morse remarked.

McLain took a sip and then said, "Whatever the captain says. Thanks, man."

Morse just smiled and gave him a wink. He then put his cup down between his legs and added, "And this captain feels like flying," and switched the plane off auto, took the wheel, and continued his journey.

"Whatever you say."

McLain was fine with that and took a large swig of coffee. It was good, so he took another.

Then, little by little, he began to gasp for air, heaving for a breath like a man on death row without the row. McLain looked at Morse, whose smile was wide and happy. Three times he gasped for air, holding his throat, just as a commotion from the cabin began. Cries of choking could be heard, as well as loud-voiced, gargled sounds and then pounding on the cockpit door. In the cockpit, McLain looked to Morse once more as the coffee fell to the floor, and he fell to the side of his seat. It was over, and the cabin was over too. Eight minutes of chaos and it was done. Morse immediately placed the plane on auto again and went to check on the cabin. From the doorway, he could see all ten men strewn out in the aisle with cups on the floor, all dead.

Satisfied, Morse went back inside the cockpit, closed the door, and moved on. That smile widened with the success. His job was over. Now it was the other's turn. It wasn't over yet, but soon.

He checked the instrument panel once more and then sat back and relaxed. He had just made his pay raise.

* * *

The cloud cover had broken free just over the horizon, showing the sun's afterglow on the underbelly of the passing clouds. The isolated airfield sat quiet. Eight men stood outside the one and only hangar, four in orange jumpsuits and four in plain clothes carrying AK-47s. They were waiting for the plane.

Then, the faint sound of a jet engine could be heard in the distance just above the horizon. The men walked out a ways onto the runway, one with orange flags in his hands. Suddenly, the sound of machine guns blared their way, coming from the hangar. Seven men in ski masks who were dressed in black, looking like a special ops unit, stormed not only the hangar but also the area of the tarmac. Seven men took the area within moments. The four security men with AK-47s never knew what hit them. They were fast, and they were good.

The plane cruised in and onto the tarmac, stopping parallel to the hangar. With the plane at a stop, the seven men waited for the sign for all success. The door opened, and Morse stood in the doorway. When they saw a thumbs up, the seven got to work. Three hustled into the plane and cut the chains from the couriers while the others climbed into the fuel truck and began their task. Bodies of the dead co-pilot and the rest were thrown onto the tarmac and left. After the refueling, the seven men, plus Morse, jumped into the plane with their cargo and flew away. It was clean, simple, and well organized.

Now for the last leg.

∗ ∗ ∗

Under the cover of darkness, a truck was waiting for a plane to touch down. With a clear sky, it'd be easy to hear and see the Gulfstream touch down; they were ready. The truck was an old flatbed. They'd made a fence-style frame around the flatbed itself with a tarp roped over it. It was a regular overgrown pick up.

Soon a plane could be heard—a small plane, yet hardly a Piper. It sounded larger, and within a matter of moments, the lights from the plane could be seen. The two transporters of the truck jogged to the side of the tarmac and waited for it to touch down. The other three men under the tarp came out as they then pushed it back.

Even though you couldn't see your hand in front of your face, the lights from the small jet would suffice. This might be the first time they'd done this, but they were told exactly what to expect and what to do.

The plane landed and taxied down the short runway. As soon as the plane stopped, the lights were enough to maneuver the product quickly and easily. The men in the plane delivered the goods to the truck, and the five put the diamonds under bologna and baguettes. Later they'd be inside them. It was trite and unoriginal, but it worked. It got those diamonds on their last leg of the journey. Anyway, who would stop monks?

* * *

Toward ten o'clock p.m., DeViamond answered the library phone. He listened. A smile grew upon his face like a wide-eyed boy with a new bike. He hung up, and then looked at Sasal.

"The monks are en route."

Sasal sat back in his chair and smiled like a wolf in a flock of lambs.

Chapter Fourteen

I t'd been four days, and Rafi had been home the entire time. He didn't go to work; he just stayed with Danielle, his gun by his side as if it were a growth. It made Danielle wonder if he slept with the damn thing.

She took another sip of her wine; it was late, and Rafi had been standing in front of his windows with hands in his pockets. Danielle watched him, wondering what was so interesting besides the full moon. The atmosphere was as volatile as a Molotov cocktail. She could feel it and knew he could too. *So let's make it more volatile,* she thought.

"Tell me, Cardinel, how many people have you killed?" Danielle asked.

He stood silent, but it was that silence that made her realize it was many. She knew that wasn't what he wanted her to know.

"That many, huh?"

He turned and faced her. "In war many people die."

"I'm not talking about war."

He took a breath through his nostrils and said, "No, I didn't think you were." He walked to the table and took a seat across from her. Then he watched her put a cigarette to her lips and light it. "What would you like me to tell you?"

"For once the truth would be nice."

He watched her cigarette smoke snake to the ceiling and then looked into her eyes. "Too many. Is that what you wanted to hear?"

She looked into her wine through the glass and said, "Well, it's certainly an answer."

Rafi picked up the bottle of wine and poured himself a glass. Then he walked his wine back to the windows. "Why didn't you tell me about the book?"

Danielle ran her finger around the rim of the glass and answered, "I told you when I knew."

He did a quick 180 to look at her. "Not true!" he flatly remarked. "Boris called you. You should have told me that night!"

Danielle sighed and then took a sip of wine. She didn't want to get into it with him. Finally she said, "I didn't think there was much to tell until it arrived."

"Don't ever keep information from me again!"

Danielle narrowed her eyes. "Is that an order?"

"No, but I suggest you take it under advisement."

A knock at the door interrupted Danielle's rebuttal. Rafi went to answer, leaving his wineglass on the table as he passed by, and disappeared into the foyer. After a moment, she heard voices, one new.

Herzog walked in, followed by Rafi and another Israeli. She looked over the unfamiliar face and then realized he was at Rafi's that first night as well. He was tall and lanky. His hair was curly, and he wore a beard and mustache. Good looking—the intellectual type. Herzog was his usual self and began with introductions.

"Danielle, this is Moshe, our decoder. Moshe, Danielle." Herzog smiled that Lugar smile again. God, he loved his job.

The two nodded to one another as Danielle lifted her glass to him with a sober face. Danielle wasn't into the spirit of the party.

"Danielle," Herzog began, "Moshe is one of our code breakers— one of the best. I showed him your book. Moshe has a few findings you should know about." He then looked at Rafi as he extended his hand toward the table. "May we?"

Rafi simply nodded once as his eyes narrowed, and he picked up his wine and took a large dram. Danielle could see he was trying to soften Moshe's findings, because he wouldn't be here unless he had something. She also knew Herzog wouldn't waste time either. They all took a seat at the table except Rafi.

"Danielle," Moshe said as he opened the book, "this is encoded, but in plain English, it's a book code."

"What!" Rafi couldn't believe it. "That book can't be in code!" It was obvious he refused to postulate any thought that Sam could be involved with this.

"I'm sorry, Rafi, but it is," Moshe said as he looked at him.

"So what the hell is a book code?" Danielle asked and then sat up straighter.

"A book code is basically what it says. It's taken from a book or novel or something of reference." He turned the open book to face Danielle and pointed with his finger. "This first numbers actually looks like dates, but the other numbers could, for example, be a paragraph. The next could be a line, the next a word or letter. It all depends on the book. And that's what I need. The book."

"Which is where you come in," Herzog eagerly interjected. "We need to know the book. Can you think of any book that it may be taken from?"

Danielle took a sip of her wine as she thought and then looked at Rafi. Finally, she said, "Try *Mein Kampf.* It was Sam's favorite."

"What the hell does Sam have to do with this?" Rafi was becoming unduly upset. "The man is dead. Can't you leave him alone!"

Danielle sighed. "Cardinel, nothing in that office got by Sam. You know that as well as I. I'm sorry. It may have come from Lydia's desk, but it's Sam's book."

Rafi tried to control his anger but smacked his wineglass on the table, almost breaking the stem. "I can't believe it," he replied. "Sam wouldn't be involved with something like this. How could he be? He's dead because of it." He paused for a moment and then said, "Lydia could have gotten involved five years ago without Sam's knowledge or used him. Maybe Lydia isn't as clean as you think."

"That's a possibility," Herzog thought aloud, rubbing his chin. "But I think we'll go with Danielle's offerings." He looked at Moshe. "Go and work on it. See what transpires."

Rafi stayed silent as he looked at Danielle as if she'd betrayed him. She knew the matter was out of his hands, and she'd helped. Now he wanted nothing more to do with the book or anything else this mission had to offer, but he knew that wasn't an option, and so did Danielle.

Herzog and Moshe stood, taking the book with them. "Thank you, Danielle," Herzog said. Then he added, "Welcome to the team." That Lugar smile came back.

"Herzog, you have the compassion of a gas chamber," Danielle replied.

Herzog chuckled. He'd gotten what he'd wanted—Danielle's help.

Herzog and Moshe left, with Rafi staring Danielle down. He'd had enough, and he wanted her to know it.

Danielle got up from the table, downed her wine, and then said, "Now you know how it feels to be deceived."

With a clenched jaw, Rafi watched Danielle disappear into the bedroom hall. Civil unrest had returned.

✳ ✳ ✳

"Bloody hell!" Nibbons retorted. "A damn plane? How much money are we talking about?"

The minister of the interior remarked, "Close to a half a billion dollars."

"How?"

"Obviously very well. They must have had an insider. That's the only way it could be taken."

"I'll call Tel Aviv. They have to know."

✳ ✳ ✳

Hans and Olan walked the streets of Manhattan's diamond district as the snow fell. That evening, Forty-Seventh Street was thick with pedestrians gawking at the fine jewelry stores' windows with Christmas only three weeks away. The two kept their hands in the pockets of their leather jackets, looking like the Hardy Boys. Hans was fascinated by the snow. It wasn't as if he'd never seen it before; he'd just never seen it amongst the awesome lights of the Big Apple. He stuck his tongue out to catch a flake. When he did, boyish laughter came forth. Olan poked his elbow into Hans's side.

"It's fun," Hans said, still smiling from his catch. "You try."

"Remember why we here," Olan remarked.

"Yes," Hans said with a gleam in his eyes. Then he stuck out his tongue again. There was nothing he loved more than his job and catching snowflakes.

The two walked a half a block farther to a glass and metal door in between two store fronts. Olan looked up at the address on the glass above the door and gave Hans a nudge. Hans took out a key, placed it in the lock, turned the key, and opened the door. The shops may have been on the ground floor, but the real diamond market was above. They walked through the door, and then Hans locked it from behind. A tall staircase faced them, with two elevators in the hall facing the side of the staircase. They'd take the elevator.

On the third floor, they went directly to Goren's offices just off the elevators. After three steps they were standing in front of the door. Hans took out another key, placed it in the lock, and turned. The door opened, and they stepped in. Olan looked to the left of the door to find the security alarm engaged. He pressed the appropriate code on the panel, and the little red light at the right upper corner simply flicked. They were in. Olan looked at Hans and gave him a nod. The two unzipped their jackets, pulled their semi-automatics from their shoulder holsters, and moved on through the second door.

Down the long hall they could see a florescent light illuminated at the back; a desk sat underneath it. It seemed another hallway veered off to the right. Voices could be heard coming from there as they made their way quietly down the hall. They pulled the slides of their guns and slowly continued. Then a redheaded young man and an older, bald one came into view as the two came to the desk, their conversation continuing, obviously unaware of Olan and Hans.

Then the redhead looked down the hall. He saw them and their guns pointed at him.

"No!" Boris gasped.

Marvin stood in terror.

Hans took his shot. The bullet hit Boris directly between the eyes. He fell back against the wall and crumbled to the floor. Hans's boyish smile grew, and he gave his gun a kiss.

Olan fired and hit Marvin in the chest. Marvin simply dropped. Olan also couldn't help but show a grin.

"Now for Danielle and that book. You go there," Olan said as he pointed to Danielle's office. "I'll take this one," he added as he popped his hand on Boris's desk.

In Danielle's office, there was no Danielle. "Olan," Hans called. "Danielle not here."

"Then find the book. That's the most important ting."

Hans checked everything he could in Danielle's office, ripping through and causing as much destruction as he could. He wanted *them* to know the extent of his hate and his *mission*. But he came up empty handed and went to Boris's desk to see if Olan had found anything of use.

"It is not here." Olan was pissed. "And no Danielle."

"We go home. DeViamond and the old man will not like this," Hans muttered.

"We will have to report back. I will make the call." Olan's anger didn't allow him to think.

Olan picked up the receiver on Boris's desk and dialed. After an answer, he explained there was no book or Danielle and hung up. "We go home."

The two walked down the hall and out the door, leaving Boris and Marvin where they lay, limp and dead.

* * *

DeViamond put down the receiver back into its cradle, stunned by what he'd just heard. *Sasal will throw a fit,* he thought. He hated his outbursts. Founded or not, they were harsh with bellows that spewed forth like an overexerted mother bear protecting her young. But he had to know. He had to tell him, but that could wait until tomorrow. It was too early, and DeViamond wasn't in the mood for his bitch session. He'd wait until Sasal had a few brandies under his belt. That would, hopefully, lessen the blow.

* * *

Later that day, DeViamond walked into the great hall, where he knew Sasal would be sitting by the fire with a brandy. It was close to dusk, and now was as good a time as any to let him know of the call he'd had from Olan. He went to Sasal with a heavy heart and quite frankly, fear. Sasal was one man you didn't want to piss off; friends or not, it made no difference. He told him of the missing book and Danielle.

"How could you know so fast?" Sasal asked with suspicion in his voice as he turned to look at him.

"He called from the office."

"What!"

Oh God, DeViamond thought. "Why is that so …"

"Because it is on record!" Sasal threw his snifter into the fire, breaking it into shards.

DeViamond never thought of that and began to cower.

"Danielle must be in Israel vit Rafi. Dhe book must be vit her. Dhat's dhe only explanation." He thought a moment, his face red from anger, and then said, "Contact Mohammed and Abdul. For once dhey'll be of use. Dhey have twenty-four hours. I vant her out of dhe vay and dhat book back. Hopefully she von't know vhat dat book contains. Check every hotel in Tel Aviv, dhough I don't understand vhy she'd be vit Rafi dhis time of year." His eyes narrowed, darting back and forth as he thought. "Damn it! Someting tinks. And by dhe vay, vhat has dhe Brit said?"

"Nothing yet. But we'll keep at him. Don't worry, Sasal. We'll get something," DeViamond obediently replied. Then he went off to carry on with the task of terrorizing Somner.

"Call Mohammed first. Danielle has to be taken care of. I vant dhat book, and I don't care how I get it. Is dhat clear?"

"Of course, Sasal."

DeViamond left to do his duties as ordered.

* * *

In Haifa, Carl Jacobs looked through the lens of his high-powered microscopes at one of the diamonds from Rafi's mystery package in which he'd cut the stone in half. He examined the rings within the stone, showing its identification of origin. It was South African, just like the last batch Rafi had received. The rings, like that of a tree, grew closer together as you reached the center. He knew Rafi wouldn't be happy to hear that, for most diamonds stemmed from that region. That would leave Rafi with a lot of territory to choose his gift givers from. He'd make the call and tell him the bad news.

* * *

Rafi took the last sip of his sweet tea as he and his head cutter, Chaim, held a discussion over an uncut stone. Rafi was examining it carefully, and both agreed that two one-half carats would do nicely without losing too much ruff. The phone rang as Chaim took the stone and left his office.

Rafi picked up. "Cardinel," he said as he pushed the empty glass toward the back of his desk.

It was Carl. He told him the news. Rafi wasn't amused. Besides, the note from the package came back negative. He felt as if he were looking down a well with a single light bulb to aid his dimly shining intel, and that little bit of light he had was slipping away even faster. He hung up. With all this marvelous news, he hoped it couldn't get any worse.

It was then he thought of Danielle. She hadn't been out of the apartment for five days. He wondered how much more of this *protection* crap she'd put up with before she decked Erez and took off. He wouldn't put it past her. So far she'd been a good girl, or as good as expected. He didn't know how long that would last. A talk with Herzog about it was in order. He'd leave early and hit his office before he went home for the night.

Rafi looked at his watch. It was a little after three. There was nothing pressing in the office at that time, so he got up, slipped on his blazer, grabbed his briefcase, and left for the day.

* * *

Herzog was on the phone when Rafi stepped just inside his office. Herzog motioned for Rafi to come in, but Herzog seemed a bit out of sorts—controlled but definitely out of sorts. Rafi narrowed his eyes. He wondered what was up.

"Let the police handle it. We'll get the records," Herzog ended and put the receiver back in its cradle as he looked up at Rafi. "There was a break in last night at Goren's. Two dead."

Rafi looked at him with sheer astonishment. "What? You can't just break into a diamond company. There are too many barriers to go through!"

Herzog stood as he threw down a pen onto his desk. "Well, they did. And I suggest we don't tell Danielle ... At least not yet. Hell, she'll never trust us again."

"What do you mean again? She doesn't trust us now."

Herzog just gave Rafi a look and then picked up a piece of paper containing more intel. "You're not going to believe this. There was a call made from Goren's around the time of the break in. We don't have a trace; they weren't on long enough. But we're going to get the records. That's being done as we speak."

A young man came to the door with a large, folded note and said, "For your eyes only, sir."

Herzog walked to the door, took the note, and then waved the young man away. He opened it, read it, and then gave it to Rafi to read.

Rafi's eyes widened as he did. He then looked at Herzog as he gave the note back. "From Nibbons?"

Herzog nodded. "It seems the last DeVorhes shipment didn't make it."

"Hijacked?"

Herzog wadded up the note, put a match to it, and then tossed it in a metal wastebasket. "Hijacked." He walked back to the windows with his hands behind his back, and said, "They're bigger than I anticipated ... very well honed. They obviously have teams wherever needed." He turned and looked at Rafi. "You know what they were after at Goren's, don't you?"

Rafi just kept that emotionless face he was famous for. He didn't want to say.

"Of course you do. Whether you want to say or not, you know. One of those bullets could have easily been meant for Danielle, and you know that too."

Rafi brushed the underside of his mustache. He knew. He just didn't want to admit it. Maybe it was time. After a good moment of thought, he said, "Then they'll figure out she's here with the book."

"I know. But we'll protect her. Don't worry." He turned and looked at Rafi harshly. "And so will you, aside from your differences."

Rafi lifted a brow and then said, "She's been under house arrest for close to a week. I don't know how much longer she'll put up with this."

Herzog turned for a moment, his fingers massaging his lower lip. Finally, he said, "Take her to lunch tomorrow. Somewhere intimate but public."

Rafi thought for a moment and then said, "The Danish Tea Room in Jaffa Market. One o'clock."

Herzog nodded. "We'll be there."

"Good. I'll be home if any other creatures crawl out of the crevasses."

Herzog nodded once and said, "Tomorrow." He then waved Rafi out of his office. Anger had found him.

* * *

Mohammed picked up the ringing phone and answered, "Na'am."

DeViamond told him of his mission. A smile came to his face. Finally, work that meant money. DeViamond told him of the mission about Danielle and the book. The two would check out all the four- and five-star hotels, looking for Danielle. That would only take a couple of hours.

He hung up and looked at his partner. Abdul heard the conversation, at least from their end, and knew what was afoot. He was smiling. Mohammed nodded to him and pulled out the telephone directory for Tel Aviv. They found nothing until they called the Dan Hotel. It was a tourist type of hotel with all the amenities. A woman said that a Danielle Goren had checked in but checked out that same night.

From there, there was no sign of her, and it was the only hotel that put Danielle that close to them. It was as if she'd fallen off the face of the country. He called DeViamond back for other suggestions, and it was good that he did. The intel was that she was most likely with Rafi and to take care of things that way. Detective work was not their strong suit, but they could be effective.

* * *

Danielle was dressed in her black leather pants and a black turtleneck. That morning it was cold; the heat didn't come on until that afternoon. From the bedroom hall, the smell of heavy coffee wafted her way. She could see Rafi sipping on a small cup of Turkish coffee. He was staring out the windows of the patio doors. She wondered what he was doing home. It was ten in the morning, and he wasn't at work. Why?

Danielle watched him with a discerning eye, almost as if she didn't know him anymore. She once knew him as Mr. Mild Mannered Business in the diamond industry, not the agent from hell who could, or would, kill on a moment's notice. She crossed her arms as her shoulder sunk against the doorway's frame. A sudden morbid feeling enveloped her.

Rafi turned his head and looked at her. He must have seen her out of the corner of his eye. "Good morning, Danielle," he said.

She took a few steps from her spot of refuge and then stopped at the dining table. "What are you doing home?"

"I thought I'd take the day off. Would you like some Turkish coffee? I made it sweet. I think you'll like it." He walked to the coffee table where the tray of coffee and another small cup sat and poured the brew from a small *samovar* pot. "If you're not awake, I can promise this will do the trick."

"Thank you," she said as she looked at him rather oddly.

Something wasn't right. He was waiting on her, being gracious again, as if the night Herzog and Moshe came never existed. She couldn't help wonder if he was wearing his gun. The black sweater he wore didn't show it, but that didn't mean he didn't have it.

She walked to him and took the cup.

"Careful," he said. "It's hot."

She took the cup and then a sip. "Thank you," she said. "It's very good."

And it was. Rich and sweet—a spoon could have stood straight up in it. But it did do the trick. He was right. It was just the thing to wake you up. And she thought an espresso could wage war. It didn't have a chance.

"So what made you take the day off?" Danielle asked as she walked closer to him.

"I thought we'd go to lunch today."

She lifted an eyebrow. "I thought I wasn't allowed out of the house."

"You'll be protected, in more ways than one."

"In other words, you're still carrying."

He didn't answer, but that was all the answer she needed.

"What type of automatic do you carry?" Danielle asked as she took a seat at the table and then took another sip of coffee.

He looked at her for a moment and then answered, "A Beretta. Why do you ask?"

"Nice gun. It's well balanced with not a lot of kick."

His eyes narrowed. "You say that as if you've used one."

"No," she nonchalantly lied. "I just watch too much television."

Rafi didn't question it and finished his coffee, leaving the bottom *mud* of grounds. "Would you like to do anything before we go to lunch?" he asked as he set his cup on the tray.

"What time are we going to lunch?"

"Around one."

A gleam came to her eyes. "Do you play much chess anymore?"

Chapter Fifteen

Mohammed and Abdul had waited outside of Rafi's from across the street for twelve hours, hoping they'd have their chance at Danielle. Rafi would simply be collateral damage. Sasal wasn't fond of that idea, but if that's what it took, then that's what it took. The two had it planned to a tee. Mohammed would search the house while Abdul would follow them. And if Rafi was the only one to come out of the house, then Mohammed would take Danielle inside, but that book had to be found. Then it happened; their targets came out. They nodded to each other and then split. Mohammed took the house, and Abdul followed with his device close to his body from under his torn vest.

✳ ✳ ✳

Danielle and Rafi headed for the market three blocks away. When they reached the area, smells of coriander, cumin, and cinnamon were just a few of the fragrances enticing them. Vendors sat side by side and across from one another in the marketplace, selling everything from clothes to baklava, meats to hookahs. A bustle of activity stormed the area, with women and their buys and burros being led loaded with wares. Rafi kept an eye on everyone and everything as they passed. He looked a couple of times behind him as if he could feel someone was following but eventually turned back and continued on.

"You're being nice to me, Cardinel. Why?"

"You don't trust me?"

Danielle rolled her eyes, feeling Rafi's hand gently take the back of her neck, keeping her close. "Let's see, first you trick me into coming to Israel, then tried to coerce me into your little affair, not to mention wanting to kill me the night Herzog and Moshe came over, and you say I don't trust you?"

Rafi wanly smiled. "You took your choice."

"And you're trustworthy."

Rafi couldn't help but chuckle and then said, "This way."

He guided her to the left, and they made their way down a wider street with nothing but restaurants. Halfway down, Rafi stopped at a particular place. Danielle looked at the window. It read, "The Danish Tea Room." At the bottom corner of the window was an American Express sticker.

"Don't leave home without it," she mumbled.

Rafi's lips curled as he opened the door for her and let her pass in front of him. It reminded Danielle of Rick's American Café from the movie *Casablanca* because the room was an arch upon arch with the walls plastered in a swirling pattern. An old-style cash register sat on the end of the bar, but that was all that was from the movie. Italian pictures adorned the establishment. To say it was a first for her would be an even trade; nothing else came close. It was a true dichotomy.

"What kind of food do they chow down on in here?"

Rafi smiled wide. "Mexican."

Danielle sighed. "Only you, Cardinel. Only you."

Rafi laughed. "And you were expecting …?"

Danielle just shook her head as her eyes rolled. She was right. Only Cardinel.

A man in a white shirt and bistro apron came to them and asked as he held up two fingers, "Shtayim?"

"Ken, b'vacashah," Rafi answered yes and thank you in Hebrew.

The waiter showed the two to a table toward the middle of the room. Rafi held out a chair for Danielle and then took his own seat. The waiter placed menus in front of the two and then left.

Danielle looked at the menu, which was in Hebrew. "What do they serve?" she asked and then put her menu down on the table. She knew very little Hebrew and didn't see the point of looking.

"I told you. Mexican." Rafi smiled, waiting to see her reaction.

And what a reaction. "What! You were serious?" she softly exclaimed. "The place is called The Danish Tea Room, has Italian décor, and serves Mexican? Oh, I can already tell this is going to be a treat," she drolly remarked.

Rafi just laughed at her cynicism. "Would you like me to order for you?"

"Hell, why not? It can't get any stranger." She took another glance around the place. "As I said, only you, Cardinel. Only you."

Rafi smiled, elated he wasn't so damn predictable to her.

After a long moment of silence, Danielle's face became solemn as she took out a cigarette and lit it.

Rafi couldn't help but feel the change in her and said, "I really am sorry how I arranged to get you here."

Danielle sighed as she examined the head of her cigarette burning red. "So am I." She looked at him. "I detest lies. Sam was a plethora of lies, to name one of his few fascinating characteristics."

Rafi refused to remark on the subject. For some odd reason, he felt it might be better that way. Besides, he'd like to just stay away from it—at least for today.

Danielle looked at Rafi's pinky, on which a one-carat ruby ring proudly sat. "A present for your fortieth birthday." She then looked into his dark eyes. "I should know," she told him. "I bought it, wrapped it, and sent it, all in Sam's name."

Rafi tipped his head and looked down at it and then at her. She was telling the truth, and he knew it. It was obvious to her that he never knew, but why would he?

A waiter came to their table, interrupting their pathway through the past. In Hebrew, the waiter asked if they were ready to order. Rafi said they were and ordered tacos with refried beans and rice.

"Tov," the waiter said with a smile, took their menus, and headed for the kitchen.

Rafi looked at his ring again. "I never knew you sent it," he said and then touched her hand as his eyes met hers.

She lifted an eyebrow and said, "That year we both received memorable gifts." She slid her hand from his and pulled her sweater up. Just above her midriff showed a bullet wound on the side of her abdomen. It was old, but it was there.

Rafi's eyes narrowed, though he tried to curb his reaction to the scar. But Danielle could see his restraint was difficult.

"That was my sixteenth birthday present from Sam. Nice, isn't it?"

Rafi just looked into her eyes. Danielle could see it was the first time he truly believed her, and that was scary for him, for she was sure it made him think of all she'd said to him about Sam. It was messing with his head, and she knew he didn't know what to think.

* * *

Soon after, an Arab man in his thirties came into the restaurant, and not being formally seated, took a table not far from Rafi and Danielle. The man caught Rafi's attention and looked at him for a moment with curiosity. Even Danielle was curious. It seemed odd he wouldn't wait for a waiter to seat him, she thought. Rafi looked over at him again more intensely. The Arab fumbled with something under the table, as if placing something there. He looked at Danielle with concern, his mind churning. The man then got up and left as suddenly as he arrived. Rafi watched him leave and then looked back at the table. Suddenly Rafi grabbed Danielle's arm and pulled her up and away from the table as he said, "Time to go."

"What the …? Cardinel!"

Rafi dragged her out from the restaurant and took her up the street. When they were fifty meters away, an explosion blew through The Danish Tea Room that rocked the area like a small war zone. Rafi and Danielle were thrown to the ground. Rafi moved atop Danielle to keep her safe from the falling debris. Screams sounded as people ran in all directions but where they should. The area was a disaster, the restaurant gone along with every life in it. From one end of the street came the Israeli Defense Force, all in their khakis and Galil rifles. From the opposite end of the street came Herzog and Erez, both ends running for Danielle and Rafi.

Finally, Rafi rolled off Danielle and settled onto his knees. He picked Danielle up and took a good look at her. Seeing only minor cuts on her face and hands, he took her into his arms and held her tight.

"Danielle, tell me you're all right."

Though trembling as she held onto Rafi tight, she answered, "Shaken but not stirred."

Rafi breathed a sigh of relief and hedged a smile at her James Bond comeback. "Thank God," he whispered in her ear.

Herzog and Erez ran to Danielle and Rafi and helped them to their feet.

Rafi looked at Herzog, furious. "They found Danielle!"

"But we have the perpetrator," Herzog said. "He's in custody right now."

"How?" Rafi demanded as he kept a tight arm around Danielle's shoulders. "How could they find her!"

"Easy, Rafi," Herzog began. "We caught an Arab man running from the scene just before the blast even happened. He looked too suspicious, and Shlomo ran him down." Herzog looked at Danielle. "Are you all right, my dear?"

She just nodded her head as she took a deep breath.

Herzog looked at Rafi and said, "Take her home. Erez will follow, just to be on the safe side. I'll be there shortly."

Rafi nodded, and all three began to walk from the area, Rafi's arm around Danielle and hers around his waist. He held her tight, as she did him. The army was left with the rest of the *housekeeping*.

Chapter Sixteen

Rafi, Danielle, and Erez walked to Rafi's front door and found it ajar. Rafi looked at Erez and immediately drew his gun. "Stay with Danielle," Rafi ordered as he handed Danielle off to Erez.

"Rafi, no," said Danielle. "Wait until Herzog gets here."

"Danielle, I'll be all right. Just stay with Erez. I want you safe."

"Be careful," Danielle added.

As he reached the arched doorway, he held his gun up and looked back at Danielle and Erez, gave them a nod, and then disappeared.

Rafi held out his gun to a silent house that held a disaster. It was as if a tornado had ripped through the house. Couch cushions were on the floor and odds and ends were knocked over. He walked through the living area and then drifted into the dining area, all the while his gun at the ready.

He came to the bedroom hallway and threw his shoulder to the wall of the entrance. He made a sudden move in front of the hallway with his gun ready in front of him. Making his way down the hall, he checked each room. Nothing. He made his way back into the dining/living area and found the only thing that was in its place was the paint on the walls and the picture of the rabbi at the Wailing Wall. The bedrooms were in the same condition.

He made his way back to Erez and Danielle in the foyer, taking the stairs by twos. "It's clear," he said to Erez, and both began to help Danielle down the stairs.

Danielle held her hands up, and said, "I'm fine," and started down the stairs.

Rafi wouldn't take no for an answer and took one of her arms and walked with her. She was still trembling, but Danielle wasn't about to tell anyone of her pain. Erez followed as he put his gun away.

As they walked into the living area, Danielle gasped. Erez just looked around, shaking his head.

"Put the cushions back, Erez," Rafi said as he walked Danielle toward the couch.

"Got it," he answered and hurriedly put the upholstered cushions where they belonged.

Rafi settled Danielle on the couch and then kneeled before her to look more closely at her facial wounds. He had his own, but he was more interested in hers. He gently touched the one above her brow, and she flinched. He looked into her eyes and said, "I'm sorry."

Her eyes told him she accepted his apology. "I thought you were dead," she said softly to him.

"After eighteen years of you whispering sweet nothings in my ear, I'm now immune," he gently said and then smiled for her.

A sarcastic twinge took her lips. "Sweet talker."

"That I am," he said with a touch of seriousness in his eyes as he looked at her scrapes. He turned to Erez and said, "In the bathroom, there's peroxide and cotton balls. Get them."

"Right," Erez said and was gone to retrieve the effects.

Rafi took Danielle's hands and said, "I'm truly sorry about this, Danielle."

She nodded as her eyes drifted downward.

Just then footsteps could be heard coming down the foyer stairs. Rafi pulled his gun and stood, aiming at the arched doorway. It was Herzog. An inner sigh of relief left Rafi's body as he put the gun away.

"What the hell happened in here?" Herzog asked as he looked at the disaster. Rafi's desk was even on its side.

"I had company," Rafi answered, kneeling down again. "Bad company."

Herzog stepped to Danielle and asked, "How are you doing?"

"Thanks to Cardinel, I'll live a long and fruitless life," she dryly remarked.

Rafi smiled. He was proud of her. She hadn't lost her sense of humor in spite of the bombing.

By now, most Israelis were used to the everyday battles. This being her first, she was doing damn well.

Erez finally showed with the box of cotton balls and the bottle of peroxide. Rafi took them, poured some peroxide on a cotton ball, and began to take aim at her forehead cut.

"Whoa, whoa," Danielle said as she flinched her head back and held up her hand. "I don't do pain. Where's my anesthesia?"

Rafi smiled wide and put down his cotton ball. "Erez, there's some brandy in the cupboard in the kitchen."

"Right." He headed for the kitchen as if on a deadly mission.

They heard the cupboard open and a hefty bottle put on the counter. Then there was a sound of glass crashing on the floor. "Sorry, Rafi," Erez called.

"Thank God he's better with a gun," Herzog said. He pulled off his gloves and stashed them in his coat pockets.

Erez came out with the bottle and a glass. "I'll clean up," he said as he put the two on the coffee table and then left to do his chores.

Rafi gave his head a single shake, opened the bottle, and began to pour a small amount of the amber liquid. Danielle saw what she considered to be a minuscule amount and tipped the bottle from the bottom for more. She needed it.

She looked at Rafi and said, "Anesthesia, Cardinel, anesthesia." With that said, she took a large gulp and felt the warmth of the liquor entice her soul.

Rafi sighed with a touch of humor and began to clean the cut above her eyebrow and her cheekbone scrape. It was obvious the liquor was taking effect; she didn't flinch once.

"How are you feeling?" Herzog asked with concern.

"Like a building fell on me."

Herzog smiled. "It did, my dear. It did."

"You're so helpful, Herzog."

Herzog just smiled. He then instantly dropped the smile as he announced, "Because of what happened today, things will be stepped up. I'm contacting the team. Everybody is on standby."

Erez came out of the kitchen with his broom, and after hearing Herzog, he asked, "Should I contact the group now?"

With authority and his bombastic manner, Herzog said, "Immediately."

"On it," Erez said and went for the phone, standing the broom against the fireplace.

"Danielle," began Herzog, "do you know anyone in the Netherlands?"

She looked at Rafi. "We both do. Baron Edmond DeViamond. His family business is there. Why?"

"We intercepted a call from your office in New York the night of the break in, but we couldn't pinpoint the location within that country."

"Break in! What break in?" Danielle stood.

Herzog put his hand to his chin in a pause. He then said, "Danielle, you know why Rafi's house looks the way it does, don't you?"

"They were looking for that damn book, and what break in!" Then it hit her—a call to DeViamond from the office of Goren's. Home! She then pushed Rafi's hand away and started to reach for the phone as she exclaimed, "Boris! Marvin!" But Rafi grabbed her arm to stop her.

"Danielle, don't," Rafi said and held onto her tightly, for it was fruitless.

She looked into Rafi's eyes as she narrowed hers and asked, "Why?"

She demanded to know. She had to know. But there was silence in the room, and she looked to Herzog. Then she figured it out. "They're dead, aren't they?! Tell me, damn it! Aren't they!"

She jerked her arm from Rafi's grip.

"Danielle, it's not your fault," Herzog said in a comforting tone.

Rafi took her hands and held them gently.

She took her hands back and stood to look into Herzog's eyes, but Herzog said nothing, wanting to let her have her moment of grief.

"Damn you!" she exclaimed and slapped Herzog with a mighty blow as her emotions consumed her. She turned with reddened eyes and looked at Rafi with ire. "You lied to me again, you bastard!" She then looked at all three. "You're all bastards, especially you!" she ranted as her eyes met Rafi's.

"Danielle, blame me," Herzog piped in. "I made him lie. Don't blame Rafi. Blame me, if you must. But it was for your own good."

"Bullshit!" she retorted and threw her glass into the fireplace.

The glass broke with such force, as if the shards flew into the dead fireplace like her splintered emotions. She'd been mislead again, which to her was another lie. Now she trusted no one, not even Rafi. He'd been the one who'd lied to her, whether it was an order or not. He'd been the one who brokered her into a situation she now faced. Her business had been raped, and Boris and Marvin were dead. What next?

It was then the tears fell, or at least those she would allow to fall, and she hated it. She was so volatile, and never had she felt these emotions. Hate was all she could feel—hate for whoever lied to her and for whoever set the tone and carried it out. Herzog and Rafi were the guilty ones. Erez said nothing and stood as if an iron rod ran up his back. But he wasn't to blame. It was Rafi and Herzog. Tweedle Dee and Tweedle Dum, except the price was higher.

"Fuck the both of you! I'm done with you!"

"The hell you are, Danielle," Herzog told her.

"The hell I'm not!"

"Like hell you are. You want justice too badly now," Herzog told her.

"Justice is nothing more than cash flow, Herzog."

"Tell your convictions that!" Herzog told her.

Danielle could say nothing to rebut. She knew he was right.

Herzog simply turned and walked for the open archway and then turned to Rafi and said, "I'll post a couple of men. Come, Erez."

Rafi just nodded.

Herzog and Erez disappeared into the foyer. Then Rafi looked back at Danielle as they both stood in silence, listening to the sound of their footsteps ascending the staircase and out the door.

Disappointment and disgust crossed her face. She glared at Rafi for a good five seconds before she finally said, "And to think I was just beginning to like you."

Danielle pushed him out of the way, walked to the bedroom hallway, and disappeared.

Rafi felt worse than he ever thought he could. He'd lied to her, hurt her, and put her in a horrid situation. Was she right? Was that book more than Herzog felt it was? But Sam was dead. How could he be involved? And Danielle—what could he say to her? She wouldn't even be good for herself. But how could he tell her? He was afraid … afraid of what he'd have to deal with in Danielle's wrath. He wasn't a monster. He was compassionate to her plight. But Herzog was stepping up operations. Rafi didn't know how much time he had to talk to her. Hell, knowing Herzog, he could tell everyone to fly out of Tel Aviv in two hours. Rafi would talk to her but not yet. He'd wait.

＊ ＊ ＊

Danielle was standing in front of the window of her bedroom to see what she could. The stars seemed to be the action that night. With arms crossed, she felt alone—alone in a foreign country with no one to turn to. Bert was far away. Danielle wondered if she even knew of the break in. She couldn't even say what her emotions were; there was so much to take in—the explosion, the book, the mysterious break-in, but mostly the death of Boris and Marvin. Too much had happened in such a short timeframe. She felt like she was on the highway to hell.

Suddenly she felt as if she were being watched. She turned and looked at the door. It was Rafi. His shoulder was up against the doorframe, and he was watching her.

She turned back to her window and asked, "What the hell do you want?"

"Danielle, I know how you must feel. I truly mean that."

"I know you do. I realize you may be stubborn, but you do have compassion."

"Then forgive me for not telling you about it sooner."

She turned and looked at him but said nothing.

He waited for a reaction, but there was none. Maybe she was out of reactionary terms. She'd had one thing after another; she didn't have the emotions to react anymore. But he did see a shining tear run down her emotionless face, the moon giving enough light for Rafi to see.

"Danielle, talk to me, please." He walked to her.

Still with crossed arms, she turned to look straight into his eyes and said, "You lied to me, you bastard."

"Danielle …"

"And don't even begin to tell me we're even or I swear you'll be singing soprano," Danielle interrupted.

"Danielle, I know …"

"No you don't, so stop right there. Boris is dead. Marvin is dead, and you decided *not* to tell me! Screw the black book! That's why they're dead! Isn't it?"

"Well at least now you know how it feels when someone holds back information."

"Holding back information! Fuck you, Cardinel. A book in one hand and two deaths in the other. Gee," she sarcastically began within her ire, "which one seizes the day?"

"Danielle, I was afraid to tell you. I didn't know how."

She stepped over to him. "Afraid? Rafi Cardinel afraid?" She threw her hands into the air and repeated, "Afraid. Well, baby, you should be." Danielle sneered, doubled her fist, and decked him as hard as she could right across his jaw.

His head jerked back from the blow as he grabbed his jaw. He then looked at his hand and found blood. Her ring had caught him, and the blood flowed.

"Feel better?" Rafi asked, rubbing his wounds.

"No. I want more retribution, and it's going to come from you."

"Danielle," Rafi began to think aloud, "whether or not you know it, you do need me here."

"Oh, this I've got to hear." She balled up her fist and took another swing, but Rafi blocked it and held her at bay.

Danielle fought him and tried like hell to do him damage, but she was no match for his strength. Finally, she dropped her head on his chest and cried.

"Rafi, they're gone," she cried.

He let her arms go, and her arms wrapped around him tight. It was then he held her in his. She broke down. She was releasing all she'd pent up inside, and she did it with him.

"Rafi, I don't want to be alone tonight."

"Then you won't."

Rafi wrapped his arms around her, as she did him. Her tears ran down her face, and Rafi could feel each one. Then he picked her up into his arms and carried her to the bed. Gently, he laid her down then sat on the edge of the bed.

"Rafi, make love to me," Danielle softly said.

He took off his turtleneck and tossed it to the floor. He bent over and kissed her. "You're sure?"

"Yes," she whispered.

"Then I will," he said and kissed her once more.

That night they made love and then fell into a deep, deserving, sleep. The next day would come soon enough.

Chapter Seventeen

Danielle awoke in a drowsy haze. Her emotions were bailing on her. It was like a drunken stupor. Then she noticed Rafi was gone. She remembered the night before, and a gentle smile took her lips. The bonus was that instead of a twenty-dollar bill on her nightstand, there was a cup of Turkish coffee in its place. Nice.

She grabbed her robe and flung it on. Then she took the small cup in her hand and took a sip. It was just what she needed—a kick in the ass. She was ready for the day. Hell, what more could go wrong?

She picked up her cup and headed for the living area.

The house was back in order—at least the big pieces—and Rafi stood looking out the French doors at the cloudy day.

Out of the corner of his eye, he saw her, turned, and smiled.

"Good morning," Rafi said.

"Yes it is. Thanks for the coffee."

"My pleasure."

"You know you're still not off the hook for lying to me."

"Blame Herzog, but you're right. I shouldn't have lied to you."

"Would you have told me?" Danielle asked as she walked to his side.

"Yes."

"When?"

"When I thought the time was right."

"There's never a good time for death."

Rafi slightly nodded. "You're right, but it doesn't mean I don't care or understand. I've lost many on my side too, Danielle. But I am sorry."

She took a sip of coffee and nodded. "So what's today going to bring?"

"That is up to Herzog."

Then they heard a knock at the door and then footsteps coming down the stairs.

"And speaking of which," Danielle replied.

Herzog came through the open arch to the living room.

"Well, you cleaned up this mishigash fast," he noted. "Danielle, how are you today?"

"Better than you." She showed a snicker.

Herzog smiled as he walked to them. "Good … good. We have the Arab who bombed The Danish Tea Room."

"I want to see him," Danielle demanded. "I want him."

"Danielle, you don't need —"

"The hell I don't, Cardinel! The son-of-a-bitch ruined my lunch. I want to see him. Besides, I know who sent him, and I'll bet he wasn't alone. His partner ransacked your home looking for that black book."

Herzog was silent for a moment as he looked at Rafi. Rafi gave no sign either way; it was up to Herzog.

"All right. You can see him, but you better behave," Herzog ordered.

"When?"

Herzog looked at his watch. "I'll meet you both there at ten this morning. You will see him, Danielle. I promise."

"Has he admitted to the bombing?" she asked.

"No," Herzog said.

"He will," Danielle said under her breath, yet Rafi heard. "Ten o'clock. We'll be there," Danielle assured Herzog.

"Fine. The two guards in front are still there until your lock is fixed."

Rafi gave a nod.

"By the way, we leave for Amsterdam tonight at ten. Be at the airport by nine at the latest. And here are your passports. Yoseph just finished them. You two are a married couple, and it will stay this way until you are notified."

Rafi and Danielle just looked at each other. Danielle smirked, and Rafi rolled his eyes.

Herzog walked to the entry arch and then turned. "Ten this morning and no sooner."

"We'll be there," Rafi said.

Danielle knew this was for her benefit more than anything. She needed closure for something, and it wasn't going to be for Boris or Marvin. Herzog would let her have her way. She deserved it.

"What time is it?" Danielle asked.

Rafi looked at his watch. "Nine."

"Time to get dressed." Danielle left for her bedroom.

"What are you wearing?" asked Rafi.

"Well I don't have much to choose from since I only packed for three days. My leather pants and black turtleneck. I don't have much else, unless you don't mind if I go shopping."

"No shopping," Rafi said. "I don't want you in the open. Not since yesterday's event."

"There you go."

Danielle left for her bedroom.

* * *

At Mossad Headquarters, Rafi and Danielle met with Herzog at ten sharp. Danielle couldn't wait to see this man. She wanted him in the worst way.

The three entered a room with a plate-glass window. A mirror was on the other side. The place was plain, almost barren. The paint was drab, and pipes showed. It was not the Ritz by any means.

Danielle looked at the Arab through the glass, and her blood began to flow. He was sitting on a chair in the middle of the room, his hands handcuffed behind the chair.

"Has he talked?" she asked, her gaze still on the suspect.

"No," Herzog replied.

"Let me talk to him. I promise I'll make him talk."

"Danielle, you aren't going to talk to him," Rafi insisted.

"Why not?"

"You want to talk to him?" Herzog commented more than asked. "Go talk to him, but the guard stays."

Danielle smirked, seeing his sidearm. "Fine."

"Sir," Rafi said with concern on his face.

"Rafi, it's all right. Let her."

Danielle opened the door and walked in. The Arab looked at her and snickered.

Danielle stepped in front of him, the guard just behind her. *Perfect*, she thought.

Standing in front of the young Arab man, Danielle asked, "What's your name?"

He wouldn't answer. He just smirked.

"No matter. Who sent you?"

Again, the man wouldn't speak. He just kept that smirk.

Danielle wasn't going to take much more of this crap. It was then she made her move. *Fuck him,* she thought. In a split second she made a −180 turn, grabbed the guard's gun, pulled the slide, took aim, and shot the man in the leg.

The Arab yelped. Rafi and Herzog came into the room, but Herzog put his arm in front of Rafi and held his other hand up for the guard, who stayed in position.

Danielle now held the gun pointed at the man's head. "I know you know English, so who gave you this job? The next one will go between your eyes. Now who sent you!" Her voice was demanding and cruel.

Rafi balked at her demeanor, for he'd never heard or seen her this ruthless before.

"Talk, you bastard, or I swear to you, I'll shoot your dick off." Danielle took a step toward the man and lowered the gun. "At this range, I can't miss."

"Vimond," the Arab yelled after a quick moment of thought.

"You mean DeViamond?"

"Yes, yes. Vimond."

"Who else?"

"No one."

Danielle moved forward another step, her gun still in his sights.

"I swear! Only Vimond."

"Wrong. Who else!" Danielle shot a bullet past his ear.

"Okay, okay … Sasal. I swear, Sasal and Vimond."

"Who else!"

"I swear, no one. I swear!"

"Right …" she murmured. "Congratulations, you live another day," she hissed. Then she looked at Herzog and said, "Send him to medical. I got what I already knew." With that she walked away, passing Rafi and Herzog and going out the door. As she left the gun on a table next to the window, she walked through the second door and out into the hall to think. Who was this Sasal? She had to know. He was the ringmaster, not DeViamond. It sounded as if she should know the name, but she couldn't place it. Why? Where had she heard it?

Suddenly, the door flew open and Rafi was on her like white on rice. He spun her around as he held onto her top arm. "What the hell was that!"

"Oh, spare me. Like interrogations here aren't worse. I just put a bullet in his leg. He'll live. Plus I got what we needed. So what are you going to do, beat me like a rented mule!"

"Where in the hell did you learn to use a gun like that?"

She jerked her arm from his grip and said, "Contrary to popular belief, you don't live with Sam without protection."

With lowered eyebrows, Rafi just looked at her, not knowing what to say. Reading his face, she could see him question what Sam was. Hell, she had showed him a bullet wound at lunch yesterday before the fireworks.

Herzog came to the two of them and said, "Thank you, Danielle. I didn't know you knew how to use a pistol that well. This is good," he said with a smile. "Surprising, but very good. We have a new lead, and you've just been recruited."

"For what?"

The man just snickered and walked off. "Rafi will take you home," he called.

"Let's go," Danielle sneered and walked off in the same direction as Herzog.

Rafi caught up with her, grabbed her arm, and stopped her in her tracks.

"Who's Sasal?"

"The head honcho. Hell, Cardinel, DeViamond couldn't put a Chinese fire drill together. Criminy, he's a parasitic prima donna who takes orders. He doesn't give them. This Sasal is running this entire op, not the baron. I can assure you of that. Now let's go."

Rafi stood for a moment in thought about what Danielle had just said. Then he caught up with her, and the two left headquarters and drove to the Shalom Towers to Rafi's company.

In the elevator, Danielle said, "I need to call Bert and my office."

"I know. I've got an office you can use."

Danielle narrowed her eyes with curiosity. Rafi had lost his bite after her display of shooting practice. She wondered why. Did Herzog's demeanor have anything to do with it? She let out a sigh and put it out of her mind.

They stepped out of the car and into Cardinel Ltd.

"I'll take you to that office I have. You'll have all the privacy you need. I promise."

I promise? Danielle thought. What the hell was up with Cardinel? First he wanted to kill her for shooting the Arab and now he was a perfect gentleman? At least it was nice and not fighting.

He led her around to a corner office that was small and neat, with a desk, phone, and computer station.

"I'll be in my office if you need anything." Rafi left, closing the door behind him.

Danielle lifted an eyebrow after his comment and then dialed the phone. First to the office. She waited for an answer. Stan finally picked up.

"Stan, how's the business?"

"Fine, Danny," she heard from the other end.

"So you're running things I gather."

"Yeah. It's not the same though. Marvin's funeral was today. I closed the office for the day."

"I wish you hadn't, but I can understand. I wish I could have been there."

"I gave the eulogy."

Danielle sighed. "I'm sure it was moving. Thank you, Stan."

"It's all right, Danny."

"I gather that you're tying up loose ends?"

"Yeah. I'm going home here pretty soon. By the way, Goldberg is coming in tomorrow."

Her eyes brightened. "There's a package for him I hand selected. It's in the vault."

"Danny, it's covered. When are you coming home?"

"I don't know. I'll keep in touch, though."

"All right. Talk later."

"Bye, Stan."

Danielle hung up and dialed home. After not talking to Bert for a week, she was sure she was up in arms with the killings and no word from Danielle.

Danielle heard a sleepy hello on the other end.

"Bert, it's Danny."

"Danny, are you all right?"

Danielle smiled a soft smile. "Yes, I'm fine. I wanted to call you to let you know."

"It's terrible about Marvin and Boris. My God, Danny, it could have been you."

"Yeah ..." she answered, knowing the killings had been meant for her. "Look, I just wanted to touch base. I'll call when I can. I don't know when I'll be home."

"Why? What's Rafi want with you?"

"Let's just say he needs me at the moment. Good night, Bert."

"Take care, Danny. Oh, by the way, the baron's New Year's party invitation came."

"Oh goody. I can't wait."

"Call me."

"Promise."

Danielle hung up the phone. She sat for a moment in the silence, thinking—thinking of all that had happened to her in the last two weeks. It was astounding when you added it all up. Her forehead fell to her hand as her other hand drew invisible pictures on the desk.

Then Sam broke through the cobwebs. If it weren't for him, she wouldn't be in this position. But she'd get him. She'd get him if it was the last thing she did. He wasn't dead, and she knew it. She couldn't prove it, but she believed it, probably more now than ever before. *How heart wrenching,* she sarcastically thought and pounded the desk with a closed fist. She had to go through with Herzog's plan. It would bring her closer to Sam. She'd play the game, for it would only tell the truth, and the truth was better than candy on Halloween. Sam just needed to take the ghostly sheet off so she could find him. That's what she believed, and that's what she was sticking to. It was the only thing that made sense to her. So who was this Sasal?

The door of the office opened. "Danielle, is everything all right?"

"Yeah. Stan has the business covered, and Bert is beside herself with worry. Everything is normal."

He softly smiled. "Good. Erez is here to take you home."

"Rafi, just give me a gun and let me take care of myself."

"Danielle, after I saw your performance this morning, that would be a no. Erez is waiting."

"Do you know what a pain in the a—"

"Now, now. Be nice."

Danielle rolled her eyes. "Fine. But you do know you are an insufferable bastard."

"Thank you." He grinned. "Now go. I'll be home around eight."

"Why so late? We have to be at the airport at nine."

"And we'll be there. There's a couple of things I need to do."

* * *

Herzog contacted Nibbons and told him of the new player in the game—Sasal. Nibbons told Herzog about the missing DeVorhes plane and the diamonds it carried. They'd meet in Amsterdam in three days.

✴ ✴ ✴

Danielle packed her clothes—what little she had. Three days of clothes didn't go far for a two-week or so stint. And now she didn't know how much longer this would go on. It was the middle of December, and it looked like the pompous ass was still going to have his annual New Year's posh party, and his extracurricular affairs would be right under everyone's nose. That was bold, the prick. It made her wonder if Rafi had gotten his invitation yet.

She picked up her small suitcase and took it into the dining area with her purse. She picked up the passport and opened the cover. Judy Blank was her name—at least from what the passport said. Funny, she never thought of herself as a Judy. Having that document in her hand made her feel uneasy and a bit nervous. She was part of the gang now, and Herzog knew she could handle a gun. Danielle wondered if that was a good thing or not. Just as she placed the passport on the table, footsteps came down the foyer stairs, and Erez stood with gun in hand.

"Trigger happy, Erez?"

He harrumphed but kept the gun out anyway. Rafi walked in and held up a hand. Erez put the gun away, and Rafi sent him on his way home.

"I'll see you tonight," Erez remarked and then disappeared into the foyer, taking the stairs by twos.

Danielle looked at her watch. "You're early. And by the way, your door is fixed, but I left it open for you. The key is on the table. I supervised. Herzog got someone out here pretty quick."

He looked at his watch. "Good. Did you see your passport?"

"Yeah. Have you seen yours?"

He picked up the other passport from the table. "Michael Blank," he replied. He looked at Danielle with a sly grin as he reached into his jacket's side pocket. He then retrieved a black velvet box. "Well, Mrs. Blank, you should have a wedding ring, don't you think?

"I suppose," Danielle remarked.

He opened the box for her, and sitting in a gold band was a three-carat diamond.

Danielle didn't know what to say except, "A plain band would have sufficed."

"You don't like it?"

"Of course I like it. Hell, who wouldn't like it?" Danielle smiled. "You never cease to amaze me, Cardinel."

"Then it was worth it." He smiled as he brought the ring out of the box and placed it on her left ring finger.

"It even fits. How'd you know my ring size?"

"I called Bert."

Danielle wagged a finger at him. "Not fair."

"All is fair in love and war."

"Tell me about it," she said quietly off the cuff.

But Rafi heard her and chuckled. "Here," Rafi said and handed her a gold band. "Put this on my finger."

Danielle looked at him and then placed the ring on his finger.

"Now we are married."

"You're so lucky to have me, Cardinel."

"Strange, but that was what I was going to say."

Danielle looked at him with a half smirk and crossed arms. Rafi just laughed.

"Oh, not to change the subject, but did you receive your invitation to DeViamond's putrid party?"

His happiness was gone as a seriousness settled in. "Yes. It came today."

"That ass. He's going to flaunt his piracy right under our noses."

"He thinks it will make a perfect cover. Anyway, he does this every year. If he didn't, he's probably afraid people would talk."

"That is one s.o.b. I can do without."

"Me too. But we better go," Rafi said as he looked at his watch.

"So now we're married."

"Yes."

"I have to admit, Cardinel, what strange bed fellows we'll make."

Rafi laughed and then said, "Let me get my bag, and then we'll take off."

He retrieved the bag and picked up hers. They were gone.

* * *

Before Rafi and Danielle got out of the car, Rafi told Danielle, "When we walk into the airport, you're going to see everyone in the group. Pretend you don't know them, and stay by my side."

Danielle nodded, seeing the seriousness in Rafi's face. It was his tone of voice that shook her world.

They got out of the car, and Rafi grabbed the two bags. They walked to the terminal and straight for the counter of El Al Airways. They picked up their tickets, dropped off their luggage, and took a seat.

The next one to come in was Herzog. He went straight for the counter, dropped off his bag, and took a seat at the other end of the aisle. Within ten minutes, the rest of the troops came in one at a time, taking different seats. No one said a word to the others except for Danielle and Rafi. Other people came and picked up their tickets and so on. But for the team, they weren't a team—not until they reached the safe house in Amsterdam. Danielle thought it was interesting how this was all going down. She took to it like a puppy taking to his first treat. She found it a bit curious, though.

Thirty-five minutes went by as Rafi and Danielle carried on a bit of a conversation with his arm around her shoulders.

Then the boarding call was made for Amsterdam in Hebrew and then English. They stood, like everyone else taking this flight, and went through security. Then they went outside to board the plane. In three hours and thirty-one minutes, they'd be in Amsterdam.

Chapter Eighteen

O ne by one the team came into the safe house on the outskirts of Amsterdam. It was the same outskirts where DeViamond's chateau was, except he was outside the city by five kilometers. Rafi and Danielle were already there with Herzog, who was the last to arrive. Herzog gave everyone the sleeping arrangements. Everyone was doubled up, some tripled. There were four bedrooms they could use in the apartment that Herzog had appropriated. Rafi and Danielle were sleeping together. Danielle remarked, "Home sweet home."

They were to share a room, so, as the others, Rafi put their bags in their bedroom down the dog-legged hall. Danielle went into the living/dining room, took a seat on the seriously distressed couch, and then put her feet up on a poor excuse of a coffee table. She could see the galley kitchen from where she sat; it was directly in front of her, going across and not back. Three stools sat in front of the window of the kitchen. Then everyone seemed to come out and find a place to sit or stand.

"Tomorrow we begin," said Herzog. "Get some rest. You'll need it."

* * *

It was ten o'clock in the morning. Everyone was up. Noshi had made Turkish coffee for everyone from his own stash he'd packed, and Yoseph was at the market getting groceries. Danielle and Rafi were sitting on the couch while Erez, Shlomo, Noshi, and Moshe sat around the table. Avi was in the radio room. It was the fifth bedroom.

Then the door opened, and in walked Herzog with a cardboard tube in his hand.

"Shalom. I hope everyone slept well," he said as he came to the table and placed the tube atop it. "These are the floor plans to DeViamond's place. Memorize them. Danielle and I are going to go for a walk." He smiled at Danielle. It was a shifty kind of smile but a smile just the same.

She raised an eyebrow and stood. "Let me get my jacket," she said and walked back into hers and Rafi's room.

Herzog opened the tube and slid out four large pages of architectural plans.

"Where did you get these?" Erez asked as all the men stood to look.

"DeViamond's home is on the historical list. I picked it up from the library."

"I didn't think you could take those out of the building," Danielle said as she put on her black leather gloves and then zipped her jacket.

"Let's just say I borrowed them." Herzog had a grin that would make a burglar shy.

Danielle half-snickered. "Okay."

"Shall we, Danielle?" Herzog said as he extended his hand toward the door.

Danielle looked once at Rafi and then left for the door with Herzog in tow.

Danielle was curious about what Herzog wanted. She trusted him because she felt he trusted her or he wouldn't have let her get away with that stunt she pulled on the Arab man. She put her glove-covered hands inside her leather pants pockets.

The two walked a short boulevard with trees that cascaded over them like a security blanket as the snow fell.

"Danielle, you don't believe DeViamond is the head of all this, do you?"

"No."

"Why?"

She shook her head. "Herzog, DeViamond couldn't organize an egg on toast. It's this Sasal who's in charge. I'm sure of that. DeViamond's being used as well. He just doesn't know it. He's a putz, but his chateau could house at least a billion dollars' worth of stones. I'm also sure of that."

"You've given me the impression, at least from what Rafi has said, that you don't think Sam is dead."

"My security stones go missing and then end up with Rafi. My office is broken into with no trouble, and Marvin and Boris are killed. Just from that I can honestly say I truly believe the bastard is alive and somehow connected to this. Rafi would say different, but Rafi was loved by Sam."

"And what about you?"

"Herzog, I slept with a Walther under my pillow. What does that tell you of our relationship?"

"So that's how you know how to use a gun. Interesting …"

"Oh, it was a real hoot at the Goren household. Sam and I were on a constant battlefield, with Bert playing referee. But because of you, I now know why we had such a terrible relationship. I wasn't his."

There was silence for a moment as they walked. Herzog was digesting all the information. Finally he said, "Do you know who this Sasal is?"

"No, but oddly it sounds familiar. I can't place it, but I know that name from somewhere. I wish I could remember. It's like a distant memory from when I was young or something. I don't know. I'm sorry."

"Danielle, that's all right. We'll find out together."

"Maybe. We'll see."

"Danielle, one more question. Why do Rafi and you not get along that well?"

"Eighteen years ago, when Rafi's mother passed away, Sam went to the funeral, and the two have been tight ever since. To Rafi, Sam can do no wrong. He believes so blindly that Sam is dead from this diamond affair that neither you nor I can convince him otherwise. Believe me, I've tried. I even showed him a bullet wound that Sam gave me as I was running up the stairs to my bedroom to retrieve my gun. Sam is vicious if things don't go his way. Rafi never saw that side of him. I swear Rafi was the son Sam never had. I was nothing to him but a bad memory, and because of you, now I know why."

"Were you hospitalized from the wound?" Herzog asked as he stopped.

"No. He hit my side as he stood on the bottom step of the staircase. It was a through and through shot. Bert fixed me up, and that was that. I didn't see him for two weeks after that."

Herzog looked down and then at Danielle. "Let's get back. I'm sure you're cold. I know I am." He softly smiled and rubbed his hands together.

Danielle smiled back. The walk was a good walk. She could finally tell her side of the story and not feel like a bitch. Herzog was understanding, and she appreciated it. Bert was the only one who had fallen into that category until now. It was nice to have Herzog on her side.

They turned and walked back to the safe house. Herzog placed his hand on her shoulder, as if giving her a little justification.

* * *

DeViamond supervised the new chandeliers he was hanging in the great hall.

"Now be careful," he said as he looked up at the beauty they held. "More to the right."

There were fifteen chandeliers altogether, six on either side and three staggered down the middle. Sasal walked in and gave a sinister stare. They looked natural, like they belonged. Maybe this wasn't a bad idea.

"Hurry and be careful. We have five days to get these put into place," DeViamond continued as he watched the enormous fixtures be hung.

With three being ready, Sasal looked at them and smiled. What a killing he'd made. He just walked back to his office.

* * *

Herzog and Danielle walked into the safe house an hour later. Rafi immediately looked at Danielle.

"Erez, I want Danielle to carry a weapon. She's going to need it."

"Yes, sir," Erez said as he obeyed and went to his room.

"Sir, is that really necessary?" Rafi asked, not in agreement with his decision.

"Rafi, I want her to have a gun, and that's final. After her show yesterday, she can have a gun. She gained more intel than we did, and as Danielle said, he'll live."

Rafi let out a breath and looked at everyone around the table who happened to be looking back. They knew of her actions the day before. Hell, when they heard about it, it was the gossip of the day.

"What would you like, Danielle?" Erez asked.

"It doesn't matter. I can shoot almost anything."

"One Glock coming up." Erez disappeared into the hall to pick out the gun in his bedroom.

"How the hell did you guys get your weapons into the country?" Danielle asked, not believing it was so nonchalant.

"Why do you think we flew El Al? I took care of it," Herzog said as he hung his coat on the back of a dining chair. "Now let's get to these plans."

Everybody gathered to one side of the round table as Herzog rolled out the plans.

"This is the first floor. Take note and memorize."

"Herzog, this isn't right. The kitchen is on the main floor, and it doesn't show that here. How old are these?"

"I have no idea, Danielle, but these are the plans I was shown," Herzog answered.

"Let me see the bottom level where the kitchen was," Danielle said as she took off her jacket and gloves and tossed them on the end of the couch, just as Erez came in from the hallway's door.

Herzog pulled out the first page, and they looked at the belly of the chateau. Danielle looked it over very closely, but it wasn't hard to detect all; she saw that it was wrong.

"This isn't right," she told them but mainly Herzog.

"How would you know, Danielle?" Rafi piped in.

"Because I was there. Four years ago, Sam took me to DeViamond's. I can't say why in hell he did because my input into the business discussions were vetoed. I spent my time going through the house. The kitchen had been moved to the main floor, and the bottom floor was reworked. There were two rooms at the bottom of the stairs. One looked like an office. Onward and off to the right was a huge room with thick doors and padlocks. It takes up almost the entire lower level."

"Danielle, show me," Herzog said.

"Right here are the two rooms with one that looked like an office with a desk, bookshelves, and such," she explained as she pointed to what was empty space on the floor plans. "Here is the huge room I was talking about. I couldn't get in, it was locked up. But at DeViamond's you could house a billion dollars' worth of product, if not more. I'd say more."

Danielle crossed her arms and stood back with her weight on one leg.

Rafi's concern showed. "How long ago was this?"

"Like I said, four or so years ago. You really have to see it for yourself to understand it. It sits on one hundred or so acres, and cameras were all over in the trees and at the gate. It's sealed. A whole team would have a problem getting in, but not two people. By the way, there's a troll's door by the moat. It takes you to the basement. That would be the way in."

Herzog thought as he looked at Danielle. Then he said, "You and Rafi. You'll go tonight and check out the area. If you can get in, take pictures. We'll take down DeViamond and this Sasal after New Year's."

Everyone took a breath as they looked at Danielle and Rafi. They hadn't expected that. Neither did Rafi, and he instantly showed it with a dropped mouth.

"Sir, Danielle shouldn't go. She's never—"

"She's never what, Rafi? Been on a mission? Hell, she is the mission as far as I'm concerned. She knows the place, and better than you, I might add. She goes, and you'll go with her and that's final.

The rest of you I want here to listen. Avi will be on the radio." Then Herzog smiled wide. "No worries. Everything will go well."

He grabbed his coat from the chair, put it on over his short-sleeved shirt, and began to walk to the door. "I'll see you all tonight at ten. We go at midnight. Oh, and before I forget, Nibbons contacted me. DeVorhes had a plane hijacked three days ago. Keep that in mind."

And with that, Herzog was gone. Yoseph finally came back with the groceries and went directly to the kitchen.

"So we have a mission tonight," Yoseph said as he put the three bags on the counter.

Erez remarked, "Yeah. And Rafi and Danielle are point."

"Congratulations, Danielle. Herzog must really trust you."

"Either that or the man is crazy," Danielle said.

They laughed.

"You'll do fine, Danielle," Moshe remarked.

"Thanks for the vote of confidence."

Yoseph smiled as he took off his coat, coming out of the kitchen. "From what I heard of yesterday's encounter, you'll be fine."

"And I'll be with you," Rafi chimed in. Then he did the unthinkable; he threw her a wink.

Danielle half smiled.

* * *

That afternoon was quiet as the team went about their business. Avi was in the radio room readying Rafi's and Danielle's communication devices. Shlomo was looking over a newspaper. Because it was in the country's native tongue, he just looked at the pictures. Noshi was sitting on a stool that was by the kitchen's bar-like window watching Yoseph make *cholent*, a meat, bean, and potato concoction. It made him hungry. Moshe was absent from the group; he was working on the black book of numbers in his bedroom. Noshi and Erez were sitting at the table watching Danielle clean her gun as Rafi watched her from the couch with Shlomo.

"Danielle, the gun is clean," remarked Erez. "I cleaned it before we got here."

"It calms my mind, Erez. That's all," she said as she drew the small brush along the barrel slowly and methodically.

Rafi narrowed his eyes. This would be a first for her to go out on a mission. He realized she had to be a little nervous, if not scared, which she'd never express. He began to feel badly for her. He remembered his first time. It was unnerving, to say the least. Unfortunately, Herzog would make sure it wouldn't be her last. She had talent, and Herzog would make sure he got his money's worth. God only knew how much that ticked him off. Rafi felt responsible for her and her welfare. It was a combination of Herzog and him. He had orders from Herzog to get her there any way he could, and he obviously succeeded. Whatever it took, he'd protect her. It wasn't a promise; it was a threat.

Danielle peered about the apartment. Erez reminded her of a *hut-hut* kind of guy. He was always ready for whatever was out there. Serious about his job, he'd be there no matter what. Moshe was quiet and kept to himself. He was a nice guy with a methodical mind but easygoing. Yoseph seemed to be a mellow dude who knew too much about everyone, but he'd keep it a secret. Shlomo was a bit of a hothead who was controlled. Danielle liked him. She respected his control. Noshi was even tempered and laid back. He was a breath of fresh air. Rafi was Rafi. Like a dog, he was loyal to a fault. She just hoped he'd find solace when this was over. It worried Danielle.

Danielle continued to brush her gun. Rafi narrowed his eyes and stood. "Danielle," Rafi began, "come with me."

Danielle said, "All right."

She carefully put the gun down with the brush, stood, and followed Rafi into their bedroom. As they walked into the room, Rafi closed the door behind them.

"What's up, Cardinel?"

"Are you all right?"

"I'm fine," Danielle lied. "Why?"

"Just wondering."

Danielle threw him a funny look. "What's wrong Cardinel?"

Rafi hedged a moment and then said, "I'm worried about you."

"Why?"

"I just don't want anything to happen to you."

"Nothing is going to happen to me."

"I just want you to feel confident about tonight."

"Cardinel, I know you've got my back. Anyway, all we're going to do is get in, have a look see, and get out. What's so tough? There are things we need to go over about the grounds. It's important."

"We'll go over it before we go. That way the intel will be fresh."

"Cardinel, I just don't want anything to happen to *you.*"

Rafi softly smiled. "Nothing is going to happen to me. I know you'll steer us in the right direction," Rafi said as he placed his hands on her shoulders. "I promise nothing will happen to you."

Danielle softly smiled. "Yeah."

Rafi took her into his arms and then kissed her on the forehead.

It was nice having Rafi hold her. Any doubt she may have had were gone.

"I promise, Danielle, I won't let anything happen to you."

"I know. That's why I'm fine," she lied again.

He held her in his arms tighter. "Danielle …"

While he held her, she just hoped her nerves wouldn't give her feelings away. Danielle was apprehensive about tonight. But why shouldn't she be? She was out of her element. Never had she played spy versus spy. It gave her solace to know Rafi would be there for her. He was a quick study, and she felt she could trust him … now.

She knew he'd be there for her. Danielle looked into his eyes and said, "Thank you."

"For what?"

"For being you."

He smiled. "Careful, Danielle. Flattery will get you anything."

"That's because you're easy."

"Not really."

Danielle's facial features slightly skewed. "You're right. But so am I."

Just then, a quiet knock pulled them apart.

"Come in," said Rafi.

Moshe opened the door and poked his head in. He looked at Danielle. "Danielle, I need you to look at the black book."

"Sure. What is it?"

"Come to my room," Moshe said and went back into the hall.

Closely behind him, Rafi and Danielle came out of hiding, and followed him to the room he shared with Yoseph and Noshi.

They stepped inside. "This book isn't helping," he remarked as he held up *Mien Kampf.* "It doesn't make sense. I've tried it backward and forward. Nothing helped."

"Let me look at it," Danielle said.

"You've never seen this?"

"No. I gave it to Herzog still wrapped," she told Rafi.

"Take a look at it. The only thing I can figure out is the front four numbers are dates."

Danielle took the small book in hand and began to read the numbers. She narrowed her eyes.

Rafi took the book and read. "But what's the rest?"

"Product. It's all about the product," Danielle smiled, "or how much of it. My, but Sam and DeViamond have been busy."

"Danielle, you don't know it was Sam," Rafi immediately said, protecting Sam from any suspicion.

"No? Then why was it found in Lydia's desk? You know nothing ever went through that business without Sam knowing about it."

Rafi kept silent and somewhat angry. He knew, as she knew, that was a true statement, but she could tell he didn't like it.

They talked on about the book, and Danielle estimated that millions had been taken—but where? They knew when. The numbers in the middle were what she couldn't understand. That's where and when it must have happened.

"Moshe, let me see that book," Danielle remarked.

Moshe handed her the *Mien Kampf* and began going through the book from the back.

"Look, Moshe. The middle of the numbers are what you need to concentrate on. The other numbers are just that—numbers."

Danielle handed him *Mein Kampf* as well as the little leather-bound book. "Take it from after the dates but before the product."

"Thanks, Danielle. I'll get on it. But how did you know?" Moshe asked.

Danielle stood from the bed and commented, "I know Sam. I know how he thinks. Start at the back."

"Thanks, Danielle. I'll get back to you on what I find."

She gave a nod with a soft-spoken smile, turned, and walked from the room.

Rafi was behind her and asked, "What will you do now?"

"Clean my gun."

Rafi just nodded and followed her out into the living room. Danielle took her seat back and began to brush the gun.

"Still at the gun, huh?" Erez asked with a simper on his lips.

"Can't dance," Danielle answered and went back to her gun.

Erez just chuckled.

"By the way, Erez, you do have silencers, don't you?" Danielle asked.

"Yeah. Why?"

Continuing to brush the barrel of the gun, Danielle said, "Cardinel and I are going to need them." She looked at him. "That's all we need is to go in there with guns blazing. This is to be a silent mission—silent being the optimum word."

"No problem. But I'll have to clear it with Herzog."

"Screw Herzog. He'll do what I tell him to. And believe me, I have my reasons."

* * *

Danielle looked at her watch. It was ten o'clock. It was time. So where was Herzog?

Everyone was waiting in the living room except Rafi and Danielle. They were with Avi in the communications room.

"Okay. This is your communications device. It acts like a two-way radio," Avi told them but mostly Danielle. "Is that what you're wearing tonight, Danielle?"

She looked at her black leather pants, matching jacket, and black turtleneck. "Yes. Why? Is something wrong?"

Avi smiled. "Not at all. In fact, it's perfect for a recon job. Let me place this on your jacket lapel."

He stood and clipped the device to the jacket. He did the same to Rafi. He was also wearing black—black pants, black turtle neck, and a black bomber jacket. They looked like the Bobbsey twins.

Just then, they heard the front door open. Rafi stepped out to see Herzog coming through the door. He came straight into the communications room.

"They're miked up, sir."

"Good. Avi, have we done a test?"

"No. I was just going to do that."

"Go into the living room by the windows," Herzog ordered the two.

The two walked out of the room while Avi did his thing on the radio and then put his headphones on.

By the windows, Rafi said, "Testing, one two." He then gave a nod to Danielle.

"One, two," Danielle said into the piece.

Herzog showed himself and gave a thumbs up.

"Danielle," Erez said as he walked into the room, "here's your silencer, and here's Rafi's."

"Why the silencers?" Herzog asked as he came closer to Danielle.

"I didn't think you'd want a blow out at the OK Corral," she said. "If I take someone out, I sure as hell don't want anyone else to know about it. The guards are staggered on the grounds. It would be easy to take out who you need without another knowing immediately."

He nodded. "I agree. Good thinking, Danielle. Is there anything else?"

"Yes." She walked to the dining room to retrieve the tube with the plans in it. The two-radio room then followed her back into the living room and to the table. "Rafi, the cameras are in the trees here, here, and here," Danielle said as she pointed and then looked at him. "Anywhere you see a red light, duck."

Herzog laughed. "Danielle, you're priceless."

"What'd I do?"

"Nothing," he said, his laughing turning into a chuckle. "Your memory is a good thing."

"Let's hope."

"Well, since you two are the only ones going, which I'm not sure I like, when do you want to go?"

"Now." Danielle took the silencer from Erez and spun the end of it onto the barrel of her gun.

"Rafi, here's yours."

Rafi took the silencer from Erez and did the same.

"Okay." Rafi looked at Danielle. "Let's go."

"I rented a van. It's white. Here are the keys." Herzog tossed the keys to Rafi. "Good luck."

Danielle took a breath. "Luck has nothing to do with it."

Chapter Nineteen

Rafi and Danielle were driving into the unknown, or at least Danielle felt like they were. Fog was thick in the low lands. The van's headlights did nothing for visibility.

"How are you doing?" Rafi asked as Danielle looked out the windshield in silence.

"Fine. And please don't ask again."

"I just want you to be at ease."

"Cardinel, we're going to DeViamond's for a little look see. That's all."

Rafi half smirked. That was Danielle, keeping it simple. "I just don't want you—"

"Stop acting like a doting lover. We're just dropping in on DeViamond. I just hope he didn't change anything. I hate surprises."

"What would he change? And I'm not a doting lover," Rafi said as he looked at her and then back at the road.

"I don't know, but if I had that kind of product in my house I can guarantee I'd step up security."

"So would I," they heard Herzog say through their mikes. "Be careful."

"Nice to hear you join the party, Herzog," Danielle said. "How much longer 'til we hit DeViamond's?"

"Not long."

Danielle nodded.

The two sat in silence the rest of the way to DeViamond's. The chateau loomed ahead.

"Damn," Danielle remarked, checking the wall that surrounded the property.

"What?"

"Stop."

"What is it, Danielle?" Herzog chimed in.

"Not now, Herzog. Cardinel, look," Danielle said as she pointed to the wall.

"It's the wall. What about it?"

"Cardinel, there seems to be a wire going across at the top."

Rafi squinted to look. "You're right. This changes things a bit."

Danielle looked at him and said, "Ya think?" Then she thought for a moment.

"Can you get in?" Herzog radioed.

"Cardinel, how high is this van?" she asked, ignoring Herzog.

"I don't know. From the ground I'd say eight or so feet."

Danielle nodded. "We're in," she said for Herzog's benefit. "I just have to figure out how we're going to get out."

"How tall is the wall?" Herzog asked.

"It's not the wall, per se. It's the wire atop it," Rafi said.

"This could be a problem," Danielle openly thought.

"No it's not," Rafi said as he smiled at Danielle. "We'll use the roof of the van to get in."

"And a tree to get out."

Rafi nodded.

"Not bad, Cardinel. Not bad at all. You're a keeper."

"Gee, thanks, Danielle. I'll remember that," Rafi remarked.

She smiled and then said, "Pull up past the gate by fifty yards. If I remember correctly, we should be parallel to the troll's door."

Rafi nodded and did so.

"Pull up as close to the wall as you can."

Rafi did, and it was so close that Danielle couldn't get out on her side. There were no guards but around the building. It would have brought on suspicion.

"Come out on my side." Rafi opened the door and slid out.

"Really?" Danielle murmured sarcastically to herself. Then she heard chuckling on Herzog's end. "Do I have an audience, Herzog?"

"Why? Does that bother you?"

"No, not at all. The more the merrier," she said and rolled her eyes.

Danielle slid out behind Rafi, who had already climbed on top of the van's roof.

"Here," he said as he extended his hand.

Danielle climbed atop the hood and then took Rafi's hand to get on the roof. She noticed the binoculars around his neck and said, "Let me take a look."

Rafi handed her the piece, and she took a look through as she kneeled atop the van.

"What do you see?"

"A lot of trees and a few guards with very big guns. Let's go."

She put the binoculars around her neck and stepped across to the wall. She carefully stepped over the wire and then jumped down by six feet. She waited for Rafi. Then she saw him—in the air, diving over the wall, and then hitting the ground in a tuck and roll. He stood.

"I'm impressed, Cardinel. What were you, a gymnast in a previous life?"

"You're sweet. But no, paratroopers."

"Hinky," she said, smirking. "This way, and watch out for the red lights."

Rafi followed Danielle between the trees, staying low for now, and then she pointed out a camera in a tree. Its red light was glowing as if it were a one-eyed tattle tale. They got to the tree line and stayed back in the shadows of a pine. Danielle saw a new addition.

"Rafi," she said in a low voice and pointed to the lamp post to the west, with a spotlight shining down on the open property ahead. "That's new too."

Rafi took the binoculars from Danielle and took a look.

"How many guards?" Danielle asked.

"I count seven. Two are by the troll's door."

"See those bushes up ahead?"

"Yeah."

"That's where we're headed. No man's land; we'll be out in the open, but it'll put us close to the door by the moat."

Rafi nodded.

"I'll go first."

Rafi grabbed Danielle's arm. "Why?"

"So *you* can protect *me* from the guards!"

"Fine. Go, then."

Danielle stayed as low to the ground as possible as she slinked to the brush.

Rafi saw a guard look their way.

"Drop," Rafi said in his mike.

Danielle lay flat on the ground as Rafi looked out over the guards. Nothing. She was safe.

"Go," Rafi said and watched Danielle take off again, this time making it to the brush.

Now it was his turn.

He stayed low, and within a few minutes he was beside Danielle.

Danielle noticed something ahead in the moat, but she couldn't see as well as she'd like through the milder fog. "Let me see your binoculars."

Rafi handed her the piece again, and she took a look.

"What the hell? Who are these guys?"

Rafi took back the binoculars and saw hooded men in small, canoe-like boats. They stopped at the troll's door, where two men were stationed, and then moved on. They stayed at the troll's door for no more than thirty seconds. Each boat seemed to be three minutes apart.

"Rafi, that's how they're getting the product into DeViamond's."

"By monks. Who would ever suspect a monk?"

Danielle sarcastically said, "That's beautiful. I couldn't come up with anything more devious."

"Hold," Herzog said through their mikes.

At the safe house, Herzog had Avi were conducting a satellite search on the computer.

"There sir," Avi said, pointing to a building five or so kilometers away from DeViamond's, with waterways meeting DeViamond's.

Herzog asked Danielle and Rafi, "How many boats?"

"Too many to count. They just seem to keep coming," Rafi answered in his mike.

"There must be another waterway that connects to the moat," Danielle remarked.

Herzog said, "There is. Come home."

As they made their way back through no-man's land, they heard a man yelling about their progress in his own tongue.

"Shit," Danielle hissed, knowing they'd been seen. She brought out her gun, as did Rafi.

They ran from the brush with the light upon them. Machine gun shots rang out.

"Head for the trees," Rafi told her.

Danielle stopped and fired. A guard dropped. She shot again as Rafi grabbed her other arm. Rafi then fired from in front of Danielle, taking another guard. Danielle fired twice more and then ducked under the trees, but they kept coming. Danielle knelt down and shot. Another guard fell. Danielle could see it.

"Good job, Danielle," said Rafi. "Now let's go!"

The two ran through the trees and ended with little resistance except gunfire as they found the van, climbed up a tree, and climbed over the wall. They jumped to the roof of the van and dropped to the ground. They could still hear gunshots. Danielle slid in, with Rafi behind her.

The door shut, the key ignited the engine, and they were off. Rafi pulled a 180 as shots were fired into the back of the van, but they were history.

Mission accomplished.

✳ ✳ ✳

Danielle and Rafi walked into the safe house and were met by the team and Herzog with cheers and a, "Good job, Danielle." Danielle didn't know or care who it came from.

She began to walk through them and said, "Yeah, I'm a real fucking hero."

The cheers were silenced as they watched Danielle walk through the living room and into the hall. Then they heard a door shut.

"What happened?" Herzog asked Rafi.

"She killed two guards tonight. I don't think that's having a good effect on her."

"Go talk to her."

Rafi nodded and went to ease some of the pain.

* * *

Danielle unzipped her jacket and threw her gloves on the bed as she thought about the night's activities. She'd shot not one but two men tonight. So how should she feel? She didn't have an answer for that. In a way she felt sad, yet mad, but most of all numb. *They were shooting at me and Cardinel,* she thought. So what was she supposed to do? Let them kill her and Cardinel? Since that was out of the question, she decided she was more mad than sad: mad for being put in that position, sad for those she killed, and numb for Herzog putting her in that position in the first place. But she knew DeViamond's grounds. It just proved that a little information was dangerous.

A knock at the door broke her concentration. She said, "Come in, Cardinel."

The door opened. "How did you know it was me?" he asked.

"Who else would come to dry my eyes? Herzog?" she remarked with her back to him.

He came in and closed the door. "Danielle, if there's anything I can do—"

"There isn't," she interrupted. "The job is done. Life goes on and la dee dah."

He walked to her and put his hands on her shoulders. "Danielle, I know how you feel."

She abruptly turned and looked him straight in the eyes. "Do you? Do you really? How many men have you killed? Ten, twenty? You see, it doesn't matter. It was a job ... that's all. I just hope that's the end of my shooting days."

"It is. The next time you'll be at DeViamond's will be at his party."

"That's what you say now." She paused and walked to the window to look out into the night and then turned to face him. "But I would like to get into that basement and find out what the hell is being done with all those diamonds."

"Danielle ..." Rafi murmured as if to say, "Stay out of it."

"What? Don't tell me you wouldn't like to know."

"We'll find out together."

"Right ... Look, doll, I killed for you tonight. I have a right to know what's going on with the diamonds."

"I never said you didn't. You'll just have to wait until we get more intel. Now why don't you get some sleep? Things will look different in the morning, I promise."

"Maybe ... maybe not. I guess we'll have to see."

Rafi walked to her and kissed her on the forehead. "You'll see. It will be."

"And when are you coming to bed?"

"After I debrief with Herzog."

Rafi left her alone as he closed the door behind him.

Danielle ripped her jacket off and threw it at the chair in the corner. Then she fell onto the bed on her back. She lay there with all her pent-up emotions. Then, out of nowhere, tears streamed down the sides of her temples. She had killed tonight. She might have fended off Rafi, but she couldn't fend off what she was feeling as a result of killing two men. Sleep was what she needed now, but could she find it? Or would it find her? Closing her eyes to it all seemed to soften the blows she was feeling. Soon, without warning or a single yawn, Danielle fell asleep, exhausted from it all.

* * *

Rafi went into the living room and told Herzog what had happened. Danielle had killed at least two guards, and he'd killed two more.

Herzog was pleased and smiled. "So our Danielle can kill. I thought it was all you, Rafi."

"No. She shot first."

Herzog brushed his chin. "So that's why she's absent from us. She needs to work out her feelings. But she can kill. That's one in our favor."

"You're not going to ask her to kill again."

"No. But it's nice to know she can if she has to." He grabbed his coat and put it on as he said, "Tomorrow I meet with Nibbons from MI5. I'll have him take the monks and check out the monastery. I'll see you around noon." He began to walk out as he said, "Good night. All of you, get some sleep."

Rafi clenched his fists at Herzog's assessment of Danielle's situation. He'd do what it took to keep her out of that night's situation again. Herzog couldn't have her; Rafi wouldn't let him. Rafi would make sure of that.

Rafi then said to the rest of the crew, "Go to bed. I'm sure Herzog will have more tomorrow."

Good nights were said all the way around, and all the men went off to their rooms. Rafi went to his and Danielle's room and found her sprawled across the bed. From the streetlamp outside that shined in, he could see that a tear had run by her hairline. He gently wiped it away. Instead of disturbing her, he picked up her jacket from the chair, took a seat, and made that his bed for the night.

The apartment was quiet.

* * *

In a seedy side of Amsterdam, an area not even a pirate would tread, sat Herzog and his counterpart, Nibbons. They sat at a corner table with a tin light that hung low with dead light. Herzog felt it was a safe haven. Everyone stuck to their own business.

"Nibbons," Herzog began, "the ones who are transporting the diamonds are monks."

Nibbons furrowed his brow. "What? You've got to be bloody kidding."

"No. Their monastery is five or so kilometers from DeViamond's. I have conformation from two of my agents. A gun fight ensued."

"Were they hurt?"

"Thankfully, no. But that night—last night in fact—they saw monks bringing the shipments in."

Nibbons took a sip of coffee with lowered eyebrows.

Herzog could see his hamster wheel whirling. The Brits were so provincial, he thought, and the side of his mouth slipped into a grin.

"So how do you want to do this?" Nibbons asked.

"We'll pick up DeViamond on the second of January. I don't want anything to alert him until then. He's throwing a big ball for New Year's Eve. He does it every year. I have two agents going in."

"How?"

"They both happen to be in the diamond industry. They've already got the invites. They'll get around for sure, but don't do anything until the second we take down DeViamond."

"Understood. But we'll keep an eye on the monks."

"The monastery is five kilometers due west of DeViamond's. Be ready." Herzog threw back the rest of his coffee. "I'll keep in touch. Just keep surveillance on the monastery and keep me informed. They may go for another run tonight."

"If anything happens I'll call."

"You know my cell." Herzog stood. "By the way, do you know anything about Somner?"

Nibbons looked up at him, and said, "No, but I'll keep in touch."

Herzog turned and left Nibbons alone.

"Bloody monks. Jeez." Nibbons swirled what was left in his coffee, put it down, and was gone, leaving a five for their tab.

✳ ✳ ✳

It was ten o'clock in the morning, and all the team members were relaxing at the safe house except Moshe, who was making coffee. Rafi took a seat on a stool at the kitchen's bar and watched him.

"I take it Danielle is still sleeping."

"Yes. I don't expect her to wake for a while."

"She must be exhausted from last night. Emotions are more difficult to get over than physical pains."

Rafi thought of that comment. Moshe was right. Rafi agreed within himself as Moshe placed a cup of coffee in front of him. Time passed, and the team drank their coffee and wandered about. Avi was the only one absent. He was playing with his gadgets and radio.

By eleven o'clock, Danielle walked out from her room. She looked like she was hung over and felt like a train wreck.

"Danielle," Moshe said. "Coffee?"

"Please." She took a seat at the table with Erez and Shlomo.

"Coming up."

Seeing a pack of cigarettes on the table with no one's name on it, she took one, at which Rafi got up from his stool and lit it with her lighter.

"Who left the cigarettes?" Danielle asked.

"Herzog," Erez answered. "They're for you."

"Oh, wonderful. Now he's bribing me. Nice."

He held it out. "It fell out of your pocket as you slept."

"That's all I need—a Saint Bernard without the brandy."

Rafi smiled. "Herzog left them sometime yesterday."

"Here you go, Danielle," Moshe said as he placed a cup of coffee in front of her.

"God loves you, Moshe, and so do I."

Danielle took it into her hands as she had the day the will was read. It sincerely seemed it was her saving grace. Rafi noticed and smiled as he looked at her; he took a seat at the table.

"Danielle," Rafi began, "we're going shopping today."

"What the hell for?"

"DeViamond's party is in a week."

"Ah, hell," she sighed and took a large drag of her cigarette.

Rafi's smile grew. He didn't want to go anymore than she did, but they couldn't refuse either. "What time do you want to go?"

"Let me finish my coffee and cigarette, and then I'll decide. Don't rush me, please. I'm enjoying infecting my lungs at the moment, and this coffee is to die for," she said to him as she embraced her cup and then took another gulp.

"Just say when."

Just then, the door opened, and Herzog walked in like he was on a mission from God.

"I just spoke to Nibbons from MI5. They're going to take the monks and keep them under surveillance. How are you today, Danielle?"

"Still too early to tell," she answered and took another sip of coffee and a drag of her cigarette.

"I hope you slept well."

"I slept."

"Good. Your heroism is noted."

"Gee, thanks." Her sarcasm was duly doused with the smoke she exhaled.

He nodded once and said, "Today is down. Relax and get situated with the mission. I'll have more when I talk to Nibbons in forty-eight hours. But we're still going in on the second of January. Keep that in mind. No one leaves."

"Sir, Danielle and I were going to go shopping." Rafi stood.

"Why?"

"DeViamond's party is in a week and Danielle doesn't have a dress to wear, and I need a tux."

"You have my approval. Go."

"Bless you, Herzog," Danielle cynically said and gave him a tepid salute.

Herzog said, "I'm going out. There are things I need to do. I'll see you all tomorrow."

The man turned and left.

"Such a sweet man," Danielle said with sarcastic zeal.

Everyone in the apartment laughed—even Rafi.

"Only you could bring such joy to our insanity."

"Careful, Erez, or you'll fall into the realm of my fascinating doldrums." Danielle smiled.

"I think I already have."

She tipped her head. "Too bad."

"When do you want to go, Danielle?" Rafi asked.

"Let me at least get dressed."

Moshe chuckled. "Danielle, you are dressed."

She looked down. He was right. She'd forgotten about her sleeping attire. She sighed. "Let me at least brush my teeth," she said as she put out her cigarette, stood, and went to do just that.

Rafi smiled and shook his head.

Before she disappeared into the hall, she stopped, and asked Moshe, "How's the book coming?"

"Good. After I got the dates separated from the rest of the numbers, it turned out they were destinations. This had to be going on for at least five years."

"How could that be?" Danielle asked Moshe. "Wouldn't someone have noticed?"

"Not back then. It was a slow and methodical act. It was only until this year that they really pushed the envelope."

"Hmmm." She looked at Rafi. This time he wasn't smiling. "Makes sense." She left to make herself presentable.

Danielle did what she could with herself and came back into the room. "Ready?"

Rafi stood and walked to grab his coat from the rack. "Let's go."

The two were history.

✳ ✳ ✳

"Careful, now," DeViamond said as his hands flailed about. "These chandeliers need to be up in one week. No mistakes, and be careful."

Sasal watched from the sidelines as the chandeliers, all twenty-four of them, were being hung. In the ballroom, the hanging pieces reminded Sasal of DeViamond—pathetic and twinkle toed. He did like the impressive lighting, though. He found it humorous. He shook his head and walked back to his office downstairs, but he got a kick out of the dichotomy.

Chapter Twenty

Rafi and Danielle jumped off the tram and headed down the street to a cute little café.

"How about some brunch?" Rafi asked.

"I think I could stomach some food about now."

"Good. Let's try this place."

The two walked in and were told to sit where they liked. They took a small table for two close to the center of the room, and a server was there before they could even settle in.

"And what would you like?" the server said, figuring they were Americans.

"I'll have tea," Danielle said.

Rafi looked at her and then ordered coffee for himself. The server went to retrieve their orders.

"Danielle, you don't strike me as the tea-drinking type."

"And people say I don't open up."

For the first time in a long time, Rafi actually smiled wide.

"Danielle, I have to ask. Are you all right?"

"Obviously you're speaking about last night."

"Yes."

Danielle took a breath as she lit a cigarette, blew out the smoke, and said, "I'm fine." She gave a half smile. "Now can we eat?"

Rafi looked into her eyes for what she'd done the night before. She might have said she was fine, but her eyes said she wasn't. He thought it best to leave it alone.

The server came back with their drinks and took their orders—two club sandwiches. Danielle didn't notice. She was staring out the window at the passersby. Rafi was watching her. It was obvious to him that she was preoccupied, probably from the night before. He wished he could make it all go away, but that was a wish he could not have.

"So, what type of dress are you looking for?" he started the conversation.

"Oh, I don't know." She looked at him. "Something vulgar."

Rafi smiled and shook his head. Danielle smiled too.

The party was a joke. They both knew it, yet every year they went. It was more out of politeness than anything else. Like before, there'd be at least three hundred people there, all schmoozing each other with compliments about how wonderful they all looked and blessings for the new year. It was a farce, and DeViamond made it complete with his sweeping conceit. He was a real piece of work.

Rafi and Danielle had a short conversation about the party over their sandwiches. Then they left to find a dress for Danielle six blocks away. The shop was designer, and Danielle liked what she'd seen in the window. Rafi agreed, and they walked in. Immediately a woman came to them.

"Do you speak English?" Rafi asked her.

"Yes. What type of dress are you looking for?"

"It's for a formal party," Danielle told her.

"Please, follow me into the salon."

Rafi and Danielle followed the woman into a barrage of beautiful dresses. Two chairs sat on the side of a platform with a three-way mirror. Rafi took a seat in one of the chairs and watched Danielle peruse the dresses.

She went immediately for the black ones. She turned to look at Rafi.

"I suppose you're going to help me pick out my dress."

"Of course. I'm CEO of your company."

"Yeah, you wish."

Danielle picked out three possibilities, and the woman escorted her to the dressing room.

The first dress she came out with was a strapless dress with ruffles. She looked in the mirror and then at Rafi. He wrinkled his nose and shook his head. Danielle agreed. The next dress was off the shoulder. Danielle looked at Rafi, shrugged, and then shook her head. Rafi agreed with a thumbs down. The last dress was black, floor-length elegance. It had long sleeves with a side slit up to the middle of her thigh. Black beading covered the dress like little sparkling mirrors.

Danielle turned around, and Rafi smiled. She raised a thumb, and his smile widened. They had found the dress. Rafi had to admit, Danielle was a beautiful woman. He took that for granted before. Looking at her with the cut necked dress that opened to her shoulders made him realize how beautiful she really was. Of course, he could never tell her. He was afraid she'd beat on him and win.

"I'll take this one," she said.

Danielle changed back into her clothes as the woman boxed the dress properly.

Rafi paid for the dress, and they were out the door.

"Now for a tux for you."

"And you're going to pick it out."

"Of course. Fair is fair."

Rafi rolled his eyes, and they stepped into a gentleman's store a few doors down.

Rafi was easy. The first one Danielle picked out was it. Rafi tried on the tux. It had a white shirt with the tips of the collar turned up. A long tie ran to a cummerbund, and the coat was short-waisted. The pants fitted his ass and had a satin stripe down the side of each leg.

"Cardinel, you clean up well," Danielle said coyly.

"You're so sweet to put it in those terms," he said with a smile. "So, you like this one?"

"Yeah, that's the one. Now all we need are shoes."

"Shoes? We have shoes for the gentleman," the man who'd helped Rafi said.

He showed Rafi some shoes, all with a glossy shine. Rafi picked out a pair, paid for them, and asked where a shoe salon for women was. The man told them just up the street. Rafi thanked him, and they left with their boxes.

After finding the store, Danielle picked out a pair of black satin shoes. Rafi paid for them as well, and they were off.

"Now where?" Danielle asked as they left the store.

"Home?"

"Not yet, but why did you let me pick out your tux?"

"You run the company."

"Ah …"

"Now where to?"

"How 'bout a brandy?"

"I think that can be arranged."

"You do come in handy, Cardinel."

"I know."

Danielle rolled her eyes, but she was smiling. The night before was far away from her thoughts.

They found a small, pub-like lounge that exuded the old world with brick walls, wrought-iron chandeliers, and old wood. A brandy would be a nice afternoon treat, at least for Danielle, Rafi thought.

They picked a table by the wall and took a seat. A waiter came at once. Rafi ordered two brandies, and the man with a bowtie and bistro apron was off to fetch the brews.

"Thank you for getting me out of the apartment. I needed it."

Rafi smiled softly. "Sometimes a new venue is all it takes to soften the mind. Besides, you needed a dress."

Danielle smiled as she looked down at the table. "Yes, I did need a dress. I hope the party's not as farcical as it usually is."

"Don't worry. I'm sure it will be."

"You make it sound so enticing that I can't wait to go."

Rafi could only smile as the man in the bowtie brought them their brandies.

Danielle picked up her snifter and said, "To you Mr. Cardinel—a man who I never knew but am pleasantly getting to know."

"Well, thank you. And here's to the woman who I am pleasantly getting to know."

They clinked their snifters and took a sip as they peered into each other's eyes from over the rims of their glasses.

Danielle put her snifter down and asked, "So, Cardinel, what's your story? How did you become a Mossad agent?"

"In Israel everyone goes to the army after high school for no less than two years. I ended up in intelligence. To make a long story short, they—the Mossad—found me to be an asset, being in the diamond business. I could go anywhere to do a job and do business at the same time. It was a perfect cover."

Danielle tipped her head, realizing how superb the cover was. "So, what kind of jobs did you do?"

"Jobs I'd rather not discuss. Some I'm not very proud of, but an order was an order." Rafi paused for a moment as if reliving those orders and took a large dram of his brandy.

Danielle didn't quite know what to say as she watched Rafi take more than a dram and put the snifter on the table with purpose. She'd never seen him drink like that before. It was obviously a matter he'd rather not recall.

"Cardinel, there's one place I'd like to stop at."

"Where?"

"City hall. I have a gut feeling I want to check out."

Rafi looked at her most curiously. "What do you mean?"

"I don't know. I just want to check something out."

"All right. But as you Americans would say, caring is sharing."

Danielle pursed her lips as her eyes narrowed. "Let's just say it's not normal for monks to be delivery boys unless they were made to do it."

"And you think you know why."

"Yes. Shall we?"

Rafi shrugged and said, "Fine. Let's go."

Danielle downed the rest of her brandy as Rafi left money on the table.

Outside, a policeman was waving traffic, and Rafi and Danielle asked where they could find property records. He told them city hall and pointed the way. They were off.

They caught the trolley and took it into the city center. There, they jumped off and headed for the hall of records at city hall. They found the people helpful and willing to give them whatever they needed. Danielle asked for the property records.

"Do you have a name?" the woman asked.

"DeViamond," Danielle answered.

The woman brightened, and her eyes twinkled. "Baron DeViamond?"

"Yes."

"But of course. He is very well known. You know he helped the monks refurbish their monastery?"

Danielle poked Rafi in the side. "Really? No I didn't know. How giving of him."

"Oh, yes. He is a wonderful man."

"I didn't know."

The woman disappeared behind some shelves and then came out with a large book of property and its holders. "You can look at it in this room if you'd like."

"Please," said Danielle, and both followed her into a small room to the back of the hall.

The woman said, "If you need anything, please ask." She smiled.

"Actually, we do. Could you help me find the baron's property?" Danielle asked.

"But of course."

Rafi and Danielle watched the woman flip through the book until she found his property.

"Here it is," the woman said with a neat smile.

"Thank you," Danielle said, and the woman left and shut the door behind her as she left.

Danielle snickered snidely. "It's DeViamond's. Look." She pointed to the main property of the chateau.

"Okay. Now what?"

"Cardinel, look. West of the main property is where the monastery sits. It's DeViamond's land. And if that woman is right, he refurbished the monastery for the monks. As far as DeViamond was concerned, they owed him. That's why they were helping him smuggle the diamonds."

Rafi half smirked as an eyebrow raised. "Danielle, you're a genius. Are you sure you don't want to join the Mossad?" Rafi asked jokingly.

"Yeah, right …"

"Herzog has to know about this."

"Yeah think?"

"Let's go."

Rafi closed the book and picked it up as Danielle opened the door. They took it back to the woman, gave their thanks, and left.

* * *

Back at the safe house, Moshe finished Danielle's black book and seemed overtaken by it all. Erez was playing with his unloaded gun at the table as Shlomo looked through the paper. Yoseph was making Turkish coffee, and Noshi lounged on the couch asleep. Avi was in the radio room checking on electronics. Most everyone had found something to do as Rafi and Danielle walked in the door.

"Hey, you're back," Erez said as he looked up from his gun. "So let's see what you got," he added as he saw the boxes they carried.

"Not until Sunday, Erez," Danielle remarked as she walked through the living room and into her and Rafi's room.

But Erez couldn't wait and followed them into the small bedroom.

"Out, Erez," Danielle said with a smirk. "You're voyeuristic tendencies will have to wait. But do you have a small gun?"

Rafi looked at her.

"How small are we talking?"

"More than a Derringer but less than a Glock."

"How 'bout a Walther?"

"That'll do," Danielle said.

"Why do you need a gun?" Rafi asked harshly.

She held a hand to Rafi as she continued. "Is there anything you've got that would go around my thigh as a holster?"

"Now wait a minute, Danielle," Rafi remarked, continuing with an adversarial tone.

"I think I can come up with something," said Erez.

"Erez, would you excuse us for a moment?"

"He doesn't have to. I want a gun going to that party now that I know DeViamond is part of the problem. I think you're going to find more than you expect when we go."

"Danielle, how would you know?"

"My gut, Cardinel. My gut." Danielle threw her boxes on the bed and looked to Erez. "Can you do it or not?"

"Yeah, I'll see what I can come up with." Erez walked out the door knowing he didn't want to be in the middle of this one. Two alphas in one room was not a good thing.

"You aren't carrying a gun to DeViamond's," Rafi insisted.

"Why? Are you?"

"Yes, which is why you don't need to."

Rafi wouldn't hear of anything else. He hung up his tux and put his shoes on the floor of the closet.

Danielle took a hanger from the closet and tossed it on the bed. Then she unboxed her dress. Without a word, she hung her dress next to Rafi's tux and placed her shoes next to his.

"I'll take this up with Herzog," she said and walked out of the room.

As Danielle went to the table to sit down with Yoseph, Moshe came out with the black book, otherwise known as the home wrecker.

"Danielle, you need to see this," Moshe said as he watched her steal another cigarette from the pack on the table.

"What is it?" She lit her cigarette and blew out the smoke.

"Look," he began as he took a seat next to her and gave her the book. "I found they were all destinations and the number of carats they received from each courier. This went on for four years. That's when it stops."

"But this has been going on for at least five years." Danielle took another drag and blew out her smoke.

"It began to escalate in the fourth year, but that's where it ends."

"Then there's another book that deals with the last year, which is what we need to find, and I know where it is."

"Where?"

"DeViamond's."

Danielle looked up at Rafi standing in the dining area's entrance from the hallway.

Danielle and Rafi peered at one another, as if challenging the other. In Danielle's eyes, she would win; Rafi would never believe it was Sam.

Rafi watched her smoke her cigarette in silence. Knowing her, she was thinking about Sam, but Rafi knew he was dead.

All Moshe had to see was this silent sparing between Danielle and Rafi, and he said to Danielle, "Would you like a coffee?"

Danielle looked at him and then his cup. Looking at Moshe, she said, "Sure. Why not?"

Moshe went to the kitchen and made another Turkish coffee. He made it sweet for her and brought it out.

With a quiet smile, she thanked him and then said, "Tell Herzog what you found, and keep this to yourself for a while. It'll be used in the future."

"How do you know, Danielle?"

"I know. Please, just do as I ask."

Moshe nodded and then went back to his room to hide the book for safekeeping.

* * *

It was getting late in the day. It was close to dinnertime, and most of the men were becoming a tad restless—even Rafi.

Avi came out of the radio room and into the living room, and asked, "What's for dinner?"

After the cholent—their main diet since no one could cook, including Danielle—the group hung out in the living/dining area.

"Anybody want a Turkish?" Yoseph asked.

Hands went up. It was going to be one of those nights. There was nothing to do and nowhere to go. Erez took a seat at the table, along with Moshe and Noshi, while Yoseph made coffee. Avi went back into his slice of heaven with his geek gadgets, and Shlomo took the couch. Danielle grabbed a cigarette from the table, lit it, and then took a seat on one of the stools by the kitchen bar. Rafi walked to where Danielle sat and leaned a shoulder against the wall. Everyone seemed to have their place.

"There's cholent left."

Everyone looked at Moshe with an "ugh" in their hearts and then back to what they were doing.

"Just a thought." Moshe took a sip of his coffee as he walked back out into the living area and took a seat by Danielle.

"What's it like being in the diamond business?" Moshe asked.

"Tedious at best." Danielle put her cigarette out after taking a last drag.

"What do you mean?" Erez asked with curiosity.

"Well, with DeVorhes holding eighty-two to eighty-seven percent of the diamonds, they hold all the cards. That's why their business is held in London."

"What's the difference?" Erez asked. Then he motioned to Yoseph, who was serving coffee.

"Because Britain allows monopolies," Danielle explained. "The United States doesn't. And that's what they are—a monopoly. But back in the seventies, Henry Witton tried to screw them over."

"How?" asked Erez.

"I don't remember exactly what he did, but DeVorhes did screw him for about ten years as punishment for what he tried."

"Now I remember," remarked Rafi, "but I don't remember what it was about either."

"If DeVorhes is that big, how in the hell did Witton try to do it?" Moshe asked.

"Like I said," Danielle reiterated, "I can't remember what he tried to do, but it obviously didn't work and he was taken down. During those ten years, he never got the stones he wanted and therefore his business suffered. It almost destroyed him."

"They obviously don't take anything for granted." Yoseph took another sip of his coffee.

"Not when it comes to diamonds." Danielle went back to the table and took another cigarette, lit it, and then went back to her stool. "Personally, I think all our answers will be found at DeViamond's."

"And what if we don't?" Rafi asked, looking at Danielle.

"We'll find something." Danielle took another drag of her cigarette and then took a sip of her coffee.

"And if we don't?"

Danielle looked at Rafi from over her shoulder and said, "We will."

"You're so sure."

"Very," she said to Rafi. "And then some."

It was getting late, and it was time to call it a night. Erez was the first to give it up and said good night. Others followed suit. Soon the only ones left were Danielle and Rafi. Danielle switched to the table and lit another cigarette.

"Are you tired?" Rafi asked.

"No, but if you're tired, please, go. I won't be long."

"You're sure?"

Danielle smiled and answered, "Yes, Rafi, I'm fine."

Rafi, Rafi thought. *She called me Rafi, not Cardinel. What's up?* Now he was worried.

"Danielle, you—"

"Go to bed, Rafi. I won't be long."

"All right. You know where I'll be."

"Good night."

"Good night, Danielle."

✳ ✳ ✳

At DeViamond's, the old man was sitting by the fireplace in the great hall, having his nightly brandy.

"Sasal," DeViamond called as he hurried through the great hall to him, "there was gunfire last night." He was beside himself, which for him didn't take much.

"So. Vhat could dhey have seen? Guards outside?"

"Sasal, they saw the monks."

"Dhey saw notting. I vouldn't be upset."

"If you say so." He began to bite his fingernails.

"I say so. Dhey can't prove a ting."

∗ ∗ ∗

It was around eleven-thirty at night, and everything was quiet. Danielle enjoyed the silence with coffee and cigarettes and in that order. Danielle unexpectedly heard the door open and close. Herzog came around the corner and came to Danielle.

"Where is everyone?"

"Sleeping," Danielle answered.

"Wake them. Nibbons believes DeViamond has Agent Somner and needs to get him out. Nibbons doesn't trust him for this long. He could be a risk to the operation. I told him we'd do it. I want you, Rafi, Erez, and Noshi to go after him."

"Why Danielle?" Rafi asked from the hallway entrance as he looked in.

"Because she knows the lower level and you because you know the grounds. Noshi for explosives and Erez for another couple of hands."

"Who is he?" Danielle asked.

"Mathew Somner, MI5. He was kidnapped about a month or so." Herzog took off his coat and tossed it on the couch.

"Well, he'd definitely be at the chateau in that one room in the lower level, next to the office."

"Why do you think he's not with the monks?" Herzog asked Danielle.

"Because they want intel. The most a monk could do is bless him to death."

"Danielle," Herzog began, "would you be willing to go?"

"I thought you already had me on the mission."

"But would you?"

Danielle lit another cigarette and said, "Yes, since you couldn't without me. But how are you going to get in? The troll's door is the only way in from the outside, and I can tell you right now it's locked for good."

"We need Noshi," Rafi said.

"Wake him, Rafi," Herzog ordered.

Rafi disappeared down the hall.

"Noshi could blow the lock."

"Herzog, you'll bring in the troops."

"No it won't, Danielle," Noshi said. "I'll use prima-cord. If I use a little, it's like a pop. It's controlled by a detonator I hold. It's very safe and does the job."

"Wake up Erez and get dressed. We also need weapons."

"With silencers," added Danielle. "We can't wake up the children."

"Agreed," said Herzog.

Noshi left to get Erez.

"I'll wake up Avi," Danielle said and began to make her way to the radio room as it seemed the whole apartment was awake, rubbing their eyes or yawning.

"What's up?" Yoseph asked.

"A mission." Erez passed him on his way to deliver the weapons. He placed them on the table.

"Avi, get Danielle, Rafi, Erez, and Noshi ready to go," ordered Herzog.

"Yes, sir," Avi said and went back into the radio room to play gadget geek.

Rafi asked Herzog, "Does Danielle have to go?"

"I'm the map, Rafi," she interjected. "I don't trust you guys with directions. Besides, I want to check out a few notables."

"Get dressed," Herzog said to Rafi. "Meet with Avi in ten minutes. You'll be briefed before you go."

Noshi, Rafi, Erez, and Danielle went back to their rooms and readied themselves for a night of retrieval.

In Rafi's and Danielle's room, Rafi asked, "Did you tell Herzog about the monk's land and who owns it?"

"I will. So now we have to rescue a guy named Somner who we hope didn't talk."

"Yes, and I ought to shoot you for getting yourself involved," Rafi said with fire in his voice. He didn't want her to go.

"First of all, I'm the only one who knows the lower level, and second you'd better aim for my heart, Cardinal. It happens to be my least-vulnerable spot."

"Why doesn't that surprise me?" Rafi commented as he zipped up his pants.

Danielle grabbed her jacket and headed for the door. Rafi grabbed her shoulder and then turned her to face him.

"Danielle, I just don't want anything to happen to you."

Danielle placed her hand on his and said, "Nothing is going to happen to me—especially with you, Erez, and Noshi to protect me." A soft smile touched her lips. "Rafi, stop worrying about me. I'll be fine."

"Promise me."

She patted his hand and said, "I promise. Now get dressed. You know how Herzog gets. Everything is life or death with him."

"Probably because it is."

Danielle walked out of the room and went to Herzog.

"In the radio room. Avi needs to hook you up."

"Herzog, there's one thing Cardinal and I found that might make you a little softer on the monks."

"Which is?" he asked as they made their way to the radio room.

"DeViamond owns the land under the monastery and also helped rebuild the monastery. They owe him."

"So it's blackmail."

"Herzog, I don't think they're doing this out of the goodness of their hearts."

"Where did you find this out, Danielle?"

"Today when Rafi and I were out buying our clothes for Sunday. I had a feeling about this, and we checked all of DeViamond's land holdings. That's what we found."

Herzog smiled as they stopped in the doorway of Avi's room. "Good work, Danielle. Good work." He smiled, beginning to form more intel. He turned to Avi. "Hook her up."

Avi clipped the microphone receiver to her cuff, and Herzog told her to go test it.

"It's the same as last time," Avi said, and Danielle went to the opposite end of the apartment.

"One, two," Danielle said into the mike. "One, two."

Herzog motioned that it was good, and Danielle went to the table to choose a gun.

Rafi, Erez, and Noshi were checked by Avi, and all were in working order. They then picked up their guns.

Herzog asked Noshi if he had the prima-cord, which he did; they were ready to go.

"Good luck," Herzog said and they left, closing the door behind them.

* * *

In the van, Rafi drove with Noshi and Erez in the back, while Danielle sat in the passenger seat.

"So what is prima-cord?" Danielle asked.

Noshi pulled out a short white cord and began to explain. "It's quite unique." He moved closer to show Danielle. It looked like two wires going through the middle of a white cord. He continued, "Inside there is one wire, which allows me to ignite the cord, and the other is the explosive. It was invented a couple of years ago. It's a piece of ingenuity."

"That is handy. I've never heard of it," Danielle remarked, looking at the plastic cord.

"You won't unless you are military or from an agency."

"We're coming up on the chateau," Rafi informed them.

"Park in the same place," Danielle said.

Rafi parked close to the wall, or as close as he could remember from the last time.

Danielle took a breath and slowly let it out. Then she looked back at Noshi and Erez and began. "There are cameras in the trees. Watch out for red lights, and stay low. Coming back you'll have to climb a tree."

"Climb a tree?"

Danielle smiled at Noshi. "Climb a tree."

"Okay, if you say so."

Rafi said, "Everybody out."

Everyone climbed out and turned for the roof of the van. Rafi climbed up first, then Noshi and Erez, and bringing up the rear was Danielle.

"Have your weapon ready. Guards could be all over," Rafi said. Then he stepped onto the wall and over.

Noshi was next, then Erez, and then Danielle.

"Remember, stay low," Danielle said to the new recruits. "Rafi, you lead."

The four made it through the pines and found no guards on the outskirts of the tree line.

"This is interesting," Rafi said.

"Where are the guards?" asked Danielle.

"Or the monks," retorted Rafi and put the binoculars to his eyes. "It's clear. No one."

"That's because they don't need the protection anymore. Everything is in its place. Noshi, Erez, see where the bushes are ahead?" Danielle asked.

Erez nodded. "Yeah."

"That's where we're headed. I'll go first," Rafi said. "Erez and Noshi, come next. Danielle, you bring up the rear. I suggest weapons drawn." He turned and took off for brush.

One by one they made their way to the brush and then to the moat. Across from them was the troll's door.

"Danielle, how deep is this moat?" Rafi asked.

"Probably no more than three or four feet. Why?"

"I'm thinking Somner isn't going to jump across, so it'd be nice to know."

"Good point, Cardinel. Let's go." Danielle took off to get close to the moat and Rafi, Erez, and Noshi followed. "That's the door we have to get past, Noshi."

"Let's jump it. Then I'll blow the door," said Noshi.

"It can't be more than four feet across."

"Danielle, you go first," Rafi said. "Noshi, you're next, then Erez, then me. Go."

Danielle jumped the moat, then Noshi and Erez, and finally Rafi. On the other side, Noshi pulled out his prima-cord and a switchblade. He cut a small piece of the white cord and then placed it inside the lock. Holding the dead man's switch next to the cord, he pressed the red button, and it popped with a small billow of smoke. The door opened.

"Danielle, explain the inside," Rafi ordered.

Danielle began, "There's a long entry of stone walls. I want one of you on one side and on the on the side I don't know how many guards there will be, so we have both sides covered. Once inside, the room we're interested in is on the right, the second door. Somehow this is spookin' me. No guards outside … It makes me nervous."

The three nodded, and Danielle went first, followed by Rafi, Erez, and then Noshi, all with guns drawn. There seemed not to be a soul as they slowly made their way along the stone walls. As they came closer to the end of the long entry, Danielle looked to the left from the right side. There was a guard. Quickly, she fired, aiming for his shoulder. He fell down to the stone floor. Then Danielle ran to him and knocked him out with the butt of her gun. She spun around to look at the entire lower level, which was one large hallway. A door with a large padlock and chain holding it closed was toward the back, but there was no one else.

Although Danielle thought it strange there were no other guards, she looked at the three and said, "Let's go."

"Danielle, is he dead?" Rafi asked.

"No. I maimed him and then knocked him out. I'll injure but I won't kill. Not again. Down here," she said and headed down the right side to the second door. "This door."

Noshi cut another small piece of the cord and stuffed it into the lock. In a poof, the door opened. They entered.

They found a young, blond man laying on the floor. Dried blood was all over his face and on his shirt.

"Somner?" Rafi said as he went to him. Then he helped him up to a sitting position.

"Yes," Somner replied. He was limp and could barely stay conscious.

"We're Mossad. We're going to get you out. Can you walk?"

"I don't know."

"Let's go. Erez, help."

Both men picked up Somner, with his arms around each man, and headed out of the room. Danielle stayed at the door and then gave the signal that all was clear—but she looked at the padlocked door and wanted to see in.

"Noshi, can you blow that padlock?"

"Sure."

"Do it. I want to know what's in there. Cardinel, come here," Danielle said.

Rafi left Somner with Erez and came to Danielle and Noshi.

"We're going to blow the big room. I've got to see what's in there," Danielle told him. "I need to know that I'm right."

Rafi hesitated and then said, "All right, but be careful."

Noshi and Danielle jogged to the big doors about twenty-five yards away. Noshi placed the cord in the lock and blew it. The lock fell open, and the chains fell away. She opened one of the doors, took one look, and said, "Get Cardinel," to Noshi. She couldn't believe what she had found.

Rafi came to her side as Noshi took Rafi's place, and Danielle walked into the enormous room of long benches and tables. "Rafi, check this out," she said as she began to walk into the room with Rafi following. "My God. Everything you'd need to cut and polish stones is here."

As they walked through the room, they saw cleavers, cutting tools, and polishing machines. At the back of this stone-walled room were four long tables with small wires and long strips of thin metal. Danielle picked up one of the wires and inch-wide metal strip. "What do you make of this, Cardinel?"

"Everything for cutting diamonds is here, but what the metal is I have no idea. You?"

"No clue. And look at that," Danielle said as she pointed to the back at the biggest safe she'd ever seen. "The diamonds must be in there." She turned to look at him. "Could Noshi blow this?"

"No. He doesn't have enough cord, and besides, it'd wake the dead."

"Good point. Let's go."

Danielle and Rafi walked from the room and closed the doors. Then they put the chains back around the wooden handles let it lay.

"Let's get Somner," Rafi said.

They went back to his bleak room of stone walls and floor. Erez and Noshi picked up Somner and pulled him to his feet. With his arms around the two Mossad agents they left, Somner dragging his feet behind.

They all took off the way they came in. Again Danielle thought it odd there were no guards. It was not like last time. It made no sense.

They made it through the moat and then to the brush. They took a break there. Their cold, wet clothes stuck to them as if it were their own skin.

"Somner, can you move?" Rafi asked.

"I can move."

"Then I suggest we go," Danielle remarked.

"So do I," Rafi said, and both Erez and Noshi picked him up and headed for the tree line.

"I don't think it makes much difference if they see us or not. Let's just get the hell out of here," Danielle said and then led the way toward the van.

They were across from the van by the six-foot wall.

"Mathew," Danielle said as she grabbed the front of his shirt, "can you climb?"

"Are you serious?" he asked.

"Unfortunately yes. Come on, Somner, help us help you." She looked at Rafi and said, "The wire on the wall doesn't matter at this point. Mathew, climb the wall. Noshi, help him." She climbed the tree and swung over to the wall.

Noshi and Rafi both helped the man up onto the wall as Erez and Danielle perched themselves on the wall. Danielle put one leg on the wall and the other across to the van and pulled Somner up with Erez's help.

Then Rafi climbed up and took Somner's other hand. Danielle, Erez, and Rafi pulled the man up as Noshi pushed and put his feet in place. Hell, Danielle felt like they were moving dead weight.

Somner stretched his hand out to Rafi as he grabbed Danielle's hand. Danielle, Erez, and Rafi helped Somner across to the van's roof, with Noshi bringing up the rear. After they were onto the roof of the van, Rafi and Noshi helped him down to the ground. Danielle slid down herself and grabbed the keys from Rafi.

"Get him in the back," Rafi said. "Danielle drives."

Noshi, Erez, and Rafi helped Somner in the back. Rafi took his jacket off and covered Somner. Danielle drove them home.

"Herzog, mission accomplished," Danielle said as she did a 180 and then headed home.

They all heard cheers through their earpieces.

"Good job, Danielle," said Noshi.

Danielle just kept on driving, feeling the effects of what they'd just pulled off.

✳ ✳ ✳

At the safe house, Herzog had the men get Avi's bed ready for Somner so Herzog could hopefully gather any intel from him he could or find out what he'd said to his captors, if anything.

It was then that Yoseph thought of Danielle and said to Herzog, "She's good. For someone who hasn't ever done this before … She's a find."

"Yes," Herzog agreed, "she is a find." He then turned and looked at Avi. "Ask how long they'll be."

"Yes sir."

"Tonight we make him comfortable. Tomorrow we get intel and find out how strong he is at torture," said Herzog.

✳ ✳ ✳

Danielle parked the van, and the three men helped Somner out of the back. Danielle led the way as the men helped Somner up the stairs. Once in the apartment, there were more helping hands that took Somner from Rafi and Noshi and helped him take off his wet clothes and then put him into Avi's bed. Avi turned the equipment off and walked to the door as the others left. Somner was covered, with his shoes off and beside his bed. The lights were out as Avi closed the door.

Out in the living room, everyone was waiting to hear what was what, but clothes had to be changed first. When they finished, they all gathered around the table.

Noshi started to talk, but Herzog interrupted. "That was smooth. No troubles, I take it."

"Yeah, and that's what gets me," Noshi said.

"Danielle, do you have any intel to share?"

She took a breath as she picked up a cigarette from the table, lit it, and then blew out the smoke.

"Well?" Herzog asked.

"They have what they want is all I can come up with. If Sam was involved—"

"But he's dead," Rafi interrupted.

"Maybe, but if he were alive, he would have had his fun. They have what they want. They have a diamond-cutting room with a huge safe. They hurt DeVorhes where it counts, and now they'll sit back for a while. Whether or not they keep Somner is irrelevant. They're done. Now they're going to sit on the diamonds until DeViamond decides what he wants to do with them, like put them on the open market."

"What would that do?" asked Noshi.

"Depending on the take, which sounds sizable if you count how many years this has been going on, could hurt DeVorhes a great deal. All they have to do now is sit and wait for the best time to unload them. For some reason, they want to hurt DeVorhes and no one else. At least that's what I think."

They could see Herzog deep in thought as his features tighten. It made sense, yet it didn't. It was an oxymoron to be true.

"Herzog," Danielle went on, "there were no guards but one on the lower level. No monks, no nothing. They have what they want."

"But they have to hide it," Herzog remarked. "Where in the hell would they hide that amount of product?"

"Well," Moshe said, "by the book's contents, they have a tremendous amount of stones."

"And after the plane heist …" Yoseph interjected.

"They have a good amount of diamonds. Billions," Danielle said.

Rafi looked at her but said nothing.

"Why would they even do this?" Herzog asked.

"For fun. Just for fun. There's no other answer I can come up with. Unless there's an underlying squelch."

"Mmm." Herzog thought and then said, "I'll talk to Somner in the morning. We'll go from there. Go to bed. I'll be back around ten. Have him ready."

Everyone broke apart except Danielle and Rafi. Herzog was out the door, and the others were on their way back to their beds.

"So, what do you really think, Rafi?"

"I don't know right now, Danielle. I don't know."

Daniele took a drag of her cigarette and then said, "You know Sam's involved with this."

"Danielle, the man's dead. Why can't you let him be?"

Danielle recognized that tone of voice. He truly believed Sam was dead and innocent. She was done.

She put out her cigarette, stood, and said, "Good night, Cardinel. I've had it."

"Wait." Rafi walked up to her. "Why do you keep on about Sam?"

She didn't say anything. She just shook her head, turned, and walked to their room. She refused to get into a fight. He truly was the grievance committee, and right now she didn't need a committee. She'd leave Rafi to his own discretions.

Chapter Twenty-One

All was serene. Rafi was looking out the window at the blue sky and the blue of the shadowed snow their building cast. Erez was drinking a cup of coffee with Danielle at the table. Yoseph finally made it out of bed, and Noshi and Avi were in the radio room checking on Somner. Moshe was in the kitchen rummaging for who knows what, and he actually could not have cared less; he was just rummaging. Boredom had taken him, and it was only nine-thirty in the morning.

Just then, Herzog came through the door. He went directly to the radio room. Seeing the two agents, he snapped his fingers, and they left at once. Herzog stepped closer to Somner. He was breathing shallowly but was alive. He'd wait.

He walked to the table and remarked, "We'll give Mr. Somner until noon. Then I'll talk to him. I'll go get Nibbons. I'm sure he'd want to talk to the young man too." He headed for the door as he called, "If he awakes, make him comfortable." And with that, he was gone.

"Tell me that man is not on meth," Danielle remarked as she blew her smoke out.

"He's not on meth," Rafi answered.

"Gee, that's such a relief ..." Danielle took another drag of her cigarette. Partially out of curiosity, but more out of concern, she got up and headed for the radio room to check on Somner for herself.

She had helped rescue him, and she felt it was her duty. When she reached his room, she turned and looked at him. Dried blood covered his face. She'd clean him up.

After getting a pan of warm water and a small towel, she began to wipe the blood away by dipping the towel into the water, wringing it out, and gently wiping the dark red streaks and blotches away. Rafi stood by the door and looked in.

"Danielle, you'll wake him."

"And what if I do, Cardinel? He needs to be presentable and awake when Herzog and Nibbons come back. If he awakes, it might not be such a bad thing. It'd give him a little time to acclimate himself to being a free man. Frankly, I'd like to hear what he has to say myself."

"Why?"

"Self-interest."

"Why? What do you expect to hear?"

"Whatever he has to say, Cardinel."

Rafi said nothing and finally left.

As Danielle wiped the blood from his face as gently as possible, she looked at him. The deep purples around his eyes, cheeks, and forehead did nothing to make the absence of blood seem any better. A prize fighter never looked so good. Taking off the blood only made him look raw. It was only an act of futility. Danielle heard groan. Somner was waking up. He slowly opened his eyes and looked at Danielle. A soft smile perched upon her lips.

"Who are you?" Somner asked in a weak voice.

"I'm Danielle. I helped get you out of the chateau last night. Do you remember?"

He looked at her for a moment with his blue eyes and smiled a bit. "Yes, I remember. You pulled me over the wall."

She lifted an eyebrow as her lips curled. "You have a good memory."

"No. You're just the prettiest one of the bunch."

"What else do you remember, Mr. Somner?"

"Mathew, please, Danielle."

"What else do you remember?"

"I'm not sure—except for the beatings. Are you interrogating me? Because if you are, I'd rather talk of other things with such a beautiful woman as yourself."

"Mathew, at noon Nibbons and Herzog will want a debriefing from you. You have to be ready."

"What time is it now?"

"About a quarter to ten. Would you like something to drink?"

"Yes. I could use a drink," he barely verbalized.

"I'll get you something. How about some water?"

"Yeah, that sounds good."

Danielle winked and gave his shoulders a squeeze. "I'll be back."

Danielle went back out into the main room and into the kitchen to fetch a glass of water.

Rafi came to her and asked, "Who's that for?"

"Somner. He's awake and cleaned up. He's foggy and having a hard time. I'll talk to him."

"Why you?"

"Because I'm not as scary as a man. He needs to get his shit together, and I don't think another man would be the right thing at the moment."

"And who put you in charge?" Rafi sternly asked.

"Look," Danielle began as she turned to look at him, "it's how it is, Rafi. What? You want to nurse him back to health so he'll be ready for his debriefing? Fine. Have at it. But he doesn't need another man to badger him right now. He'll have enough of that in the near future. He's been through a lot. Give him a break."

"Oh, and you're the one to nurse him back to health."

"Well, I can't see you gently wiping his bloody cheeks."

He looked at her with a touch of spite but couldn't disagree with her. He watched her walk away with a glass of water in her hand.

When Danielle reached Somner, she found him sitting up and rubbing the back of his neck, the covers across his legs.

"How do you feel?" Danielle asked as she handed him his glass of water.

Mathew took a drink—a large drink.

Danielle took the glass and said, "Whoa, Mathew. A little at a time. You could cramp up."

"You're right. Thank you."

"Mathew, there's going to be some tough questions. Are you up to it?"

"Yes, Danielle. With your help, yes I am. Thank you."

"Here's your water. Drink slowly."

Mathew smiled and nodded as he took the water back into his hands.

"Your clothes have dried from last night, so whenever you want, I can get them for you. But I think you should lie down and take it easy for another hour or so."

"You're right. I do need to lie back down."

Danielle covered Mathew as he melted into his pillow and fell back asleep.

* * *

DeViamond ran with purpose into the library, where Sasal was playing bookkeeper. Sasal never even looked up, knowing who it'd be.

"Sasal, Somner is gone!"

"Yes, I know dhis."

"How can you be so blasé about it! They have him!"

"And vhat could he tell dhem? Notting."

"The lock to the cutting room was broken!" DeViamond ranted. He couldn't believe the way Sasal was taking this.

"Dhey saw notting in dhat room."

"Nothing but cutting tools and polishers!"

"And I sent our guard to dhe hospital. Everting is under control, Edmond. Stop vorrying."

DeViamond left, feeling somewhat out in the open. He disagreed with Sasal's confidence. Soon his nerves began to fray.

* * *

It was noon. Nibbons and Herzog were in with Somner—a rollicking party of intel. After an hour of sideshow guess work on Danielle's part, she wanted to know what was going on in that room.

Nibbons and Herzog said words outside Somner's room but in a tone only they could hear. Nibbons left, and Herzog came into the living area and stood for a moment as he looked at each member.

"He's out for now. Danielle, keep an eye on him. I'll be back later this afternoon. Somner will be staying with us for a while until he recovers and can go back in the field. Also, we're down until DeViamond's New Year's party. Then we'll see what Rafi and Danielle find. So relax but take care." And with that, he turned and left. The closing door was his farewell.

Everyone looked at Danielle.

"What!" she exclaimed more than asked. "Just call me Florence Nightingale." And with that she headed for Avi's room where Somner slept.

✳ ✳ ✳

Two hours later, as Danielle wiped his forehead with a cool, damp rag, Somner opened his eyes.

"Danielle," Somner said in a groggy voice.

Now it was her turn to ask a few questions—questions she needed to know the answers to. He had to know something more than what she knew already.

"Mathew, how do you feel?"

"Honestly, like bloody death."

Danielle smiled. "I'm hip to that. But I need to ask you a few questions."

He sighed and then said, "All right. What do you want to know?"

"How many names did you hear?"

"DeViamond and Sasal."

"You're sure you didn't hear Sam?"

"No. In fact, they didn't even ask me that many questions. They just beat me."

"What did you hear?"

"Whirling noises that were muffled."

"Like it was in the distance?"

"More than that. Like it was being concealed."

"Behind doors?"

"Yes, behind doors. Thick doors or something like that. I also heard loud voices. 'Hurry' is all I can remember."

"Good. I want you to get some rest time. Just yell if you need anything."

"Thanks, Danielle. You've been great." He smiled.

Danielle smiled back softly, patted him on the shoulder, and left, closing the door behind her.

Chapter Twenty-Two

Sunday evening rolled around. Somner turned out to be a good mix with the rest of the agents and healed well but still on the slow side. Danielle thought it brought an international flair to the group, and she felt a little less of a minority with his English, though his accent differentiated him from her.

Danielle and Rafi were getting ready for the night's activities at DeViamond's deranged New Year's Eve party. It seemed to make her more cynical. This was something she was not looking forward to.

"Damn it," Rafi grumbled as he tried to tie his tie. "Danielle, why do ties have to be a pain in the ass?"

She snickered. "Your hands are so delicate when it comes to the arrangements of a cut diamond but lost in a tie. I love it."

"Will you help me or not?" Rafi growled.

"Only if you zip me up, so get excited," Danielle said as she turned her back to him.

As he zipped her black-beaded dress from her lower back to the base of her neck, he smiled at the remembrance of a night in Israel.

"Thank you," Danielle said as she turned to face him.

"Now, for your tie."

He stood up straight like a hot poker, and Danielle smiled. "You don't like having someone dress you?"

"No." He looked out above her head.

"You're done." She gave it one last tug to put it into place.

"Thank you. I never could tie a tie."

"So that's why you wear turtlenecks all the time."

"No," Cardinel remarked. "It's cold outside, which reminds me." He then went to the closet, pulled out a large box, and put it on the bed. "Open it."

"No. You open it. I'm tired of getting screwed from box openings. The last time I opened one of your boxes, it was my security stones. You open it." Danielle crossed her arms and refused to move.

Rafi smiled. As he opened the box, he pulled out a full-length black mink coat.

"Rafi, that's a little much."

"It's winter, and it matches your dress."

She stepped to it, but he pulled it back and said, "But only if you promise to not wear a gun."

"A bribe? You're using my health for a bribe?"

"Please, Danielle, don't wear one."

"Fine," she said as she thought of other ways to her means. "I appreciate it, Rafi. That was very sweet of you to think of me like that." She gave him a kiss on the cheek. "Thank you. Now if you'll excuse me, I need to check my makeup." She left the room.

As she walked down the hall, she slipped into Moshe's room to retrieve the little black book. Finding it on a side table, she lifted it and put it under her garter belt just above the side slit of her dress. It was flat, hidden, and easy to get to, and she *definitely* believed she'd need to.

As she was walking out, Moshe stopped her.

"Can I help you, Danielle?" he asked.

"No, Mosh. I got what I needed," she said, smiling. "Now for my makeup."

"You look great to me," Moshe yelled as he watched Danielle walk down the hall to the bathroom. She just raised her hand and gave a wave.

* * *

It was eight-thirty. Herzog had rented a limo for Rafi and Danielle to take them to DeViamond's bash. There was one thing

Danielle could say for DeViamond—he did have a flair for the dramatic for such a parasitic prick.

As the limo drove the long drive, Danielle said, "Here we go. It's show time!"

Rafi looked at her and then said, "Be good, Danielle, but keep an eye on DeViamond."

"Frankly, I'll be keeping an eye on more than him."

"Who else?"

Danielle fell silent for a brief moment and then said, "Let's get this over with. I can only stay nauseous for so long."

Rafi smiled an understanding smile. "Easy, Danielle. And remember that you're Mrs. Rafi Cardinel."

"Even here?" Danielle was puzzled.

"Especially here. DeViamond will have a definite comment, and we need to hear it."

"This should be fun. His face will fall into his lap."

"I'm counting on it. Two diamond houses coming together? As you once said, this will be rich."

"And more than shocking. And to think, Rafi, we hate each other."

"Danielle ..."

She just smiled.

The limo stopped.

"Time to make an impression," Rafi said as he looked into Danielle's dark eyes. He turned his head to the front and said, "Driver."

The driver got out of the limo and came around to the passenger's side to open the door for them. Rafi got out first and extended his hand for Danielle to take. The driver closed the door and went back to the driver's side to park. Rafi and Danielle walked to the front door. A tuxedo-dressed man opened the door, let them in, and took Danielle's fur. It seemed the minute they walked in, an overwhelming whoosh of decadence came over them. The champagne flowed, along with the outrageous amount of jewels the partygoers enveloped themselves in. Faux laughter and well wishing dripped liked blood from a suicide resting in a hot bath. They just stood in the long hall and watched the civilized mayhem in front of them down the five steps to the great room.

The first thing Danielle noticed were the chandeliers. They were a new addition, and she commented to Rafi, "Check out the lights."

"I noticed."

"Criminy, even that's a little over the top for DeViamond."

"I agree." Rafi then took two flutes of champagne from a butler passing by and handed one to Danielle.

"And to think, this is only the great room. I wonder what other incidentals there are."

"Let's go find out."

"Lead on."

"We have to find DeViamond."

"That should be easy. Just find the one with the audacious mouth."

Rafi smiled with approval of Danielle's summation. "Let's check out the ballroom."

"One of my favorite rooms." Danielle snickered.

Rafi just rolled his eyes and snickered as he escorted Danielle through the sea of people. Then he was stopped by Ruthy Hubbord, a flaky diamond heiress. She had inherited the business from her dead husband and was one of the best gossipers money could buy.

"Rafi, Danielle," she responded, somewhat startled. "You're both looking so wonderful," she added as if she'd seen a sight she'd never seen before—the two of them together.

"Thank you, Ruthy," Rafi said.

"So how have the two of you been? It's been so long." She was definitely surprised to see them together.

"We've been fine, dear," Danielle said.

"Yes," Rafi agreed. "In fact, we just got married not long ago."

Her eyes widened, knowing their history, and she said, "Really? Well, this is a call for celebration. Here's to the both of you." She lifted her glass and pinged both Danielle's and Rafi's glasses. Then she took a large drink herself. "Does the baron know about this?"

"No, but I'm sure he'll find out soon enough." Danielle smiled. She knew if this albatross of a woman knew, the whole place would know within a matter of minutes. She was famous for relishing information. Danielle knew the whole place would know before she and Rafi could even announce it. *What luck*, Danielle thought. "Well, we should be finding our host."

"Of course. I'm sure we'll see each other later."

Ruthy's smile injected a false hope of surprise, but it didn't matter. It's what they wanted. Now for DeViamond.

They made their way through the crowd with cordial consideration. It took them at least an hour and a half just to make it through the crowd. Somehow it seemed longer than that.

With that ordeal over, they made their way to the ballroom down the hall and to the left without too much trouble, though there were looks of scandal wherever they went. They were now the hot topic of conversation, thanks in part to dear Ruthy. Another hour went by.

In the ballroom, the first thing Danielle and Rafi noticed were more of those chandeliers.

"Rafi …"

"I see."

"Criminy, this is worse than the murals he had done for last year's bash."

"There's no accounting for taste."

"What taste, Rafi?"

"You have a point."

Danielle took a gulp of her drink as people said their "It's so good to see the both of you" blurbs. The BS was so deep, Danielle wished she would have worn her boots. Everyone knew how she and Rafi felt about each other, but now? They were the talk of the party.

They found DeViamond his effervescent self as they caught sight of him from the side of the room, not far from the orchestra. He was surrounded by women and a few husbands. There was laughter and gaiety. Then he looked in Rafi's and Danielle's direction but kept talking to his guests. It was a gift he had—talking out of the side of his mouth while looking for a way out through the corner of his eye.

Danielle couldn't help but look up at the chandeliers in the ballroom and remembered those in the great room. Hell, this place was turning into a brothel instead of just a whore hotel, and with their dimness, it only added to the degenerate feel. Even though they were dimly lit, Danielle narrowed her eyes at them. She'd never seen crystals cut that way for a chandelier. It somehow didn't sit very well with her, but then there wasn't that much that did when it came to DeViamond. Then, right on time, Ruthy ran to his side, not seeing Danielle or Rafi. She whispered in his ear. His eyes grew wide, and he looked at the two of them with quite a shudder.

"Danielle, I think they're playing our song," said Rafi as he took her hand and led her onto the dance floor. A strange look came over her features, but she followed him just the same.

"Rafi …" Danielle began, not understanding what he was up to. "What are you doing?"

"Watch DeViamond. We're giving him time to make his move."

And he did. Off to the side he leaned into a muscled man in a tux standing by the wall and whispered in his ear, but Danielle knew they weren't sweet nothings. He then was on the move. The two of them watched the muscled man disappear around a corner. Danielle saw it was a door. It was thin, but a door opened and closed from a panel. Rafi saw it too. Danielle looked up at the chandeliers once more, and then it hit her.

"Rafi, the crystals in the chandeliers."

"What about them?"

"Look at them! Rafi, they're octahedrons," she quietly exclaimed.

He looked at them again and found she was right. They were the first step of the cutting of diamonds.

"My God," Rafi sighed with shock. "The diamonds are the chandeliers."

"Remember the big room with the wire hooks and inch metal sheets?"

"Now we know what they were used for."

"Ya think?" Danielle said. "Now can we take him down?"

"No. We have to know who Sasal is. Keep dancing. It's close to midnight. We have to be here."

DeViamond made his way to the orchestra's stage. "Everyone! It's almost time to cheer the New Year, so take your champagne and get ready. And we also have an announcement to make."

Rafi looked at Danielle, and Danielle narrowed her eyes at DeViamond.

"Please raise your glasses to the newlyweds, Rafi and Danielle Cardinel!"

Glasses were raised as Rafi and Danielle were caught in the middle. This was not what they had in mind—especially Danielle. She had places to go and people to see—one in particular.

But DeViamond kept on with his toast. "Here's to Danielle and Rafi. Here, here!"

The crowd yelled, "Here, here!" with their glasses raised. Then came the pats on the back on Rafi and hugs for Danielle. They were stuck until someone yelled, "Ten, nine, eight, seven, six ..."

Rafi and Danielle were not the center of attention anymore.

As the crowd got into the rest of the countdown, Danielle cut through the crowd to the thin door that DeViamond's man went through.

"Danielle, don't. Just wait."

"Since when do you wait?" Danielle retorted as she pushed Rafi out of the way. Thankfully nobody noticed but kept counting down. The hype from DeViamond took center stage, literally.

Danielle disappeared while DeViamond was involved with his festivities. Not long after, Rafi ran after her.

Danielle ran down the winding stairs and then down the long hall that backed the great room. At the end of the hall were stairs going down to the right to the main floor of the lower level.

She ran past the room Somner was held in, went to the open office, and ran in. And there, before her was ...

"Sam." Her voice was not surprised. "You look pretty good for a dead guy."

Rafi stopped and leaned a shoulder against the wall to listen with disbelief. It was like a blast from the past that shouldn't be. To see Sam at the desk melted Rafi's heart—but he had lied to him. He had lied to everyone. But …

"You! You're supposed to be dead." Sam pounded a fist on his desk.

"Well, Mohammed and friend didn't do a good job. I'd fire him if it were me."

"You never change. You're still that hardnosed bitch I left."

"Some things change, Sam, and some things don't. Kind of like you. Sasal, huh. That's new."

"Dhat's my name. Sasal Gornsky. Dhat's the name I had before America changed it."

"Well, Sasal, I thought you might be needing this." Rafi watched Danielle take the black book from her garter and toss it onto his desk.

"You did have it!"

Rafi saw Sam sitting behind his desk with Danielle standing to his front. But Sam was dead. *My God,* he thought. *Danielle was right this whole time.*

"You know, Sam, I knew you were too smart to die. So who'd you kill in your place? Some homeless guy?"

"No. Your father, Abe Stern."

Rafi could see Danielle standing there in shock and awe. She didn't know what to say except to ball up her fists. "You bastard," she cried as she remembered the man and his kindness.

Rafi was having his own dilemma. Sam was alive—the man who'd taught him so much. Danielle was right, but how did she know? He didn't know what to think or how to feel. His father figure was there and alive. A myriad of emotions took hold.

"Abe Stern was my father?"

"Your modder was dating us bot but decided to pick me. Unfortunately, she laid wit him and begot you. It wasn't hard to figure out, when you came so early and healty, who you belonged to."

"You bastard." Danielle wished she had that gun to kill him, though he deserved worse.

"So what are you going to tell Rafi?"

"Dhe truth."

"The truth. Like you're such a good bet for the truth."

"Rafi is my son. I took him under my wing and taught him the business. If it weren't for me, he wouldn't be where he is, or be here at all, for dhat matter."

"But you left him!" Danielle blurted. "No wonder he was your hero and I was nothing."

Rafi closed his eyes as he leaned against the wall, not believing what he was hearing. Sam was his father. But his mother said he was dead. The numbers were right, which he figured out as he ran them through his mind. His birth date, his age ... *My God,* he thought again. A rush of disbelief and hurt overwhelmed him. It was as if he couldn't move.

"His modder was my first love. When I left Israel, I didn't know she was pregnant. Dhen I found out. She told me in a letter but told me she told Rafi I was dead. But Rafi is my son."

Rafi didn't know what to think, what to feel, or even what to accept. His father was alive and ...

"But everything you've done will be for naught," Danielle hissed.

"Not if I have anyting to do wit it."

Sam pulled a gun from his desk drawer and aimed it at Danielle.

"So now you're going to shoot me?"

"I've killed once. I can do it again. But wit you it will be a pleasure."

Rafi heard the gun cock and pulled his. Then he rushed in to be by Danielle's side. "Sam, don't!"

"Rafi!" Sam was now in shock.

"By the way, Sam, Rafi's Mossad."

Sam yelled and pulled the trigger at Danielle. At the same time, Rafi pulled his and shot. Danielle fell to the floor, and Sam fell to his desktop, dead.

Danielle hurried herself back to a standing position and looked at Rafi. Never had she seen such a look on his face. It was a look of shock and remorse all at the same time. He'd killed his own father to save her, and thank God she was safe. He could see it.

Rafi dropped the gun, turned, and ran.

"Rafi …" she called after him, but he was gone. She had to find him, but maybe it would be best to let him go. The truth can be a mighty sword.

∗ ∗ ∗

The next day, DeViamond was picked up. The diamonds were also collected, intact, and Sam's body was placed in a bag.

"Herzog, have you found Rafi?"

"No, Danielle. I suspect we won't for a while. He killed his father to save you. Everything he thought was true was not. He has a lot to think about."

"I'll run his business until he decides to surface."

"And what about your business?"

Danielle sighed. "I'll have to fly back and forth. I'll be in Israel every two weeks and New York the other two weeks."

A coroner wheeled Sam's body out and up the stairs.

"What a screw up. And Rafi heard it all, Herzog."

"I know. Let him go. He'll be back."

"When?"

Chapter Twenty-Three

Danielle had been taking care of both her and Rafi's businesses for four months. She was exhausted. She should have been used to it by now, but the jet lag did her in every time. Paperwork had piled up, and she was behind in new cuts for the diamonds for both hers and Rafi's company.

Then the phone rang. She picked up. "Danielle."

"Danielle, Herzog. Have you heard from Rafi?"

"No. Have you?"

"No."

"Damn. I'm really beginning to worry about him."

"Don't. He has a lot to think about. Let him think. He'll be back."

"I know, but when? Look, I don't mean to be rude, but I'm really behind in everything. Can I call you later?"

"That's fine. Good-bye, Danielle. And don't worry."

"I'll try. Bye, Herzog." Danielle sighed. She wanted to throw all the paperwork on the floor and call it a day. "Damn, Rafi, I wish you were here."

"I am."

Danielle looked in the doorway and was shocked at what she saw. "Rafi ..." Danielle stood from her chair from behind his desk and walked to be with him. "Are you all right?"

"I am now."

He walked toward her as she walked to him. She couldn't stand it and wrapped her arms around him, as he did her.

"Rafi, I'm sorry."

"There's no need. I finally accepted it. I should have listened to you."

"No. You did what you believed." She looked deep into his eyes.

"But you knew better. But enough. I'd rather put it behind us."

She backed away. "What do you mean us?"

He picked up her left hand and saw she hadn't taken off the ring he'd given her. He looked at her. "You're still wearing my ring."

"And …"

"Let's make it real."

"Cardinel, are you proposing to me?" she snickered.

"I am."

She crossed her arms with a smirk on her lips. "Well, I don't know. What's in it for me?"

Rafi smiled. "A fairly good-looking man who owns a shitty car and lies at times."

She laughed.

"Yes would be an acceptable answer." He smiled.

"I don't know. That shitty car is a real game changer."

"But it works." Rafi took her hand and said, "Well?"

Danielle's smirk grew into a smile. "I don't know. I have to think about it," she said as her eyes followed his smile. "Okay … yes."

Rafi smiled wide, took her in his arms, and kissed her like he'd kissed no one before.

It was over and done with. Both of them came to the realization that the past few months were now behind them. DeViamond and Sam were just as much in the past, and they didn't want to remember them at all. It was over and done. Now they had each other, and that was just fine.